## Feltner

n Feltner
in Virginia
. 1858

## Coulter

Letitia McGown === Nathan Coulter

Jefferson Feltner

Jonas Thomasson Coulter

Mason Catlett === Elizabeth Coulter

Noah Coulter

Mary Coulter

James Coulter

Parthenia B.
b. 1835
d. 1917
=== George Washington Coulter
b. 1826
d. 1889

Ernest Finley
b. 1894
d. 1945

Thad Coulter
b. 1855
d. 1912

Will Catlett

Whit Humston

David Coulter
b. 1860
d. 1938
=== Zelma Humston

Abner Coulter

Martha Elizabeth Coulter
b. 1895

Jarrat Coulter
b. 1891
d. 1967

Burley Coulter
b. 1895
d. 1977
=== Kate Helen Branch
d. 1950

Virgil Feltner
b. 1915
d. 1945
=== Hannah Steadman
b. 1922
=== Nathan Coulter
b. 1924
d. 2000

Tom Coulter
b. 1922
d. 1943

Lyda
b. 1933
=== Danny Branch
b. 1932

Mathew Burley Coulter
b. 1950

Caleb Coulter
b. 1952

Will Branch
b. 1955

Royal Branch

Coulter Branch

Fount Branch

Reuben Branch

Rachel Branch

Rosie Branch

# MARCE CATLETT:

*The Force of a Story*

Other Fiction by
# Wendell Berry

*Nathan Coulter: A Novel*

*A Place on Earth: A Novel*

*The Memory of Old Jack*

*The Wild Birds: Six Stories of the
Port William Membership*

*Remembering: A Novel*

*Fidelity: Five Stories*

*Watch with Me: And Six Other Stories of the
Yet-Remembered Ptolemy Proudfoot and His Wife,
Miss Minnie, Née Quinch*

*A World Lost: A Novel*

*Jayber Crow: A Novel*

*Hannah Coulter: A Novel*

*That Distant Land: The Collected Stories*

*Andy Catlett: Early Travels*

*A Place in Time: Twenty Stories of the
Port William Membership*

*How It Went: Thirteen More Stories of the
Port William Membership*

# MARCE CATLETT:

*The Force of a Story*

A PORT WILLIAM NOVEL

Wendell Berry

COUNTERPOINT ✣ CALIFORNIA

This is a work of fiction. All of the characters, organizations, and events portrayed in this novel are either products of the author's imagination or are used fictitiously.

Copyright © 2025 by Wendell Berry

All rights reserved under domestic and international copyright. Outside of fair use (such as quoting within a book review), no part of this publication may be reproduced, stored in a retrieval system, or transmitted in any form or by any means, electronic, mechanical, photocopying, recording, or otherwise, without the written permission of the publisher. Additionally, no part of this book may be used or reproduced in any manner for the purpose of training artificial intelligence technologies or systems. For permissions, please contact the publisher.

First Counterpoint edition: 2025

Library of Congress Cataloging-in-Publication Data
Names: Berry, Wendell, 1934- author
Title: Marce Catlett : the force of a story : a Port William novel / Wendell Berry.
Description: First Counterpoint edition. | California : Counterpoint, 2025.
Identifiers: LCCN 2025010267 | ISBN 9781640097759 hardcover | ISBN 9781640097766 ebook
Subjects: LCGFT: Pastoral fiction | Novels
Classification: LCC PS3552.E75 M37 2025 | DDC 813/.54—dc23/eng/20250310
LC record available at https://lccn.loc.gov/2025010267

*Jacket design by Nicole Caputo*
*Jacket photographs © iStock / Patrick Jennings / William Reagan*
*Book design by Laura Berry*
*Map and genealogy designed by Molly O'Halloran*
*Genealogy prepared by David S. McCowen*

COUNTERPOINT
Los Angeles and San Francisco, CA
www.counterpointpress.com

Printed in the United States of America

1 3 5 7 9 10 8 6 4 2

*To the members of my family who are still here, still at work.*

# CONTENTS

*The Past* . . . . . . . . . . . . 3
*The Future* . . . . . . . . . . . 33
    I. . . . . . . . . . . . . 35
    II. . . . . . . . . . . . . 43
    III. . . . . . . . . . . . . 55
    IV. . . . . . . . . . . . . 57
    V. . . . . . . . . . . . . 63
    VI. . . . . . . . . . . . . 71
    VII. . . . . . . . . . . . . 83
    VIII. . . . . . . . . . . . . 87
    IX. . . . . . . . . . . . . 93
    X. . . . . . . . . . . . . 101
    XI. . . . . . . . . . . . . 109
    XII. . . . . . . . . . . . . 117
    XIII. . . . . . . . . . . . . 135
    XIV. . . . . . . . . . . . . 141
    XV. . . . . . . . . . . . . 147
*Acknowledgments* . . . . . . . 153

# MARCE CATLETT:

*The Force of a Story*

# The Past

GROWN OLD, ANDY CATLETT HAS STILL AHEAD of him and in obligation the story of a time a hundred and eighteen years ago. That was early in his father's seventh year, before his father knew for sure his name was Wheeler and not "Wheeler boy," as he had so far been called and as he would still be called by some of his older clients when, down at the county seat, he sat inside an upstairs window bearing the legend

WHEELER CATLETT
ATTORNEY AT LAW

## MARCE CATLETT

They ate their supper at the swaybacked kitchen table—the young Wheeler; his parents, Dorie and Marcellus; and Andrew, his brother, five years older. The table cleared, the dishes washed and put away, they left the fire in the kitchen stove to burn out, which it soon would do, and went through the cold hall, carrying the lighted oil lamp into the living room, where they took their customary places near to the large heating stove that held fire night and day all winter.

The two boys sat at either side of the small table where their father had set the lamp, so they would have light to do their lessons for the next day. Their mother opened her sewing basket on her lap and stretched a fretted sock heel over her darning egg. She would be near enough to the boys to keep them at their work. Or try to. Wheeler had a quick mind and liked to use it. He had already submitted to a principle he would insist upon all his long life: "Study your lessons." His brother, whom he adored but could not successfully imitate, was an adept shirker. As careful of their mother as she of them, they opened their books.

Their father sat in his big rocking chair directly in front of the stove, where he could tend the fire. Often in this interval between supper and bed, he would read the Louisville paper. Or he would figure with a pencil in the small notebook, compliments of Joe

# THE FORCE OF A STORY

Moore General Merchandise, that he kept in the bib of his overalls. On that evening he did at first open the notebook. He examined for a few moments one of its pages, and then he returned it to its pocket. Rubbing the fingers of one hand slowly over the knuckles of the other, he fell into what he called "studying," by which he meant concentrated thought.

A few days ago he had finished preparing his tobacco crop for the market, prizing at last the cured and graded, appraised and cherished leaves into hogsheads that he sent by the railroad to the auction warehouse in Louisville. His final duty to that crop, before he began the first work of the next, would be to go in the morning to Louisville to see it sold and, as he thought, to receive his check.

For that reason, this would be for him a night of short sleep. The rail line between Cincinnati and Louisville passed within earshot of his own back door, but to get to Louisville in time for the sale, he would have to catch an express train that stopped only at Eagleville, ten miles away on horseback by road and then another mile or so by foot across the river on the railroad bridge. When that train whistled for the stop at Eagleville at four o'clock in the morning, Marce customarily would be building a new fire in the kitchen stove before starting his chores at the barn. But on this night he would need

## MARCE CATLETT

to be up and stirring not long after the clock on the mantelpiece struck twelve. His neighbor Jim Stedman would be waiting for him at the end of Stedman Lane, and they would make the trip together.

As he sat and thought, his silence began to weigh upon the others. It penetrated irresistibly into the hearing of Dorie, his wife, at her darning and of his sons, who were not studying but listening. Finally they looked at their mother, who was looking at their father.

"Well, Marce, what do you suppose?"

He said, looking down at his hands, "I suppose we don't know a thing for certain. I suppose if they pay us a decent price, we'll be glad of the money."

At a time when the restlessness of the frontier and the dream of something better kept people enticed and footloose, the original Catlett came into Kentucky meaning to stay. His get evidently agreed, for within three or four generations, Catletts were numerous and various in the country around Port William. When Marcellus Catlett came into his own, it was a matter of course that he would buy out the other heirs and make his life on the farm where he was born and would die. He and Dorie married, and assumed the debt on the

# THE FORCE OF A STORY

place, in the mid-1890s, a hard time that extended into the next decade. For many years they were bound and chafed by debt. It was a burden that pressed upon their land and upon their lives, so that it was felt even by their younger son.

Wheeler, who was looking at his mother, saw her face quicken with worry, and he looked again at a page of his primer without reading it.

"Yes," she said. "Whatever may be the amount, we'll be glad of the money, because we *need* it."

Marce returned her look steadily for a moment and again looked at his hands. He shook his head once to assent to the trouble in her mind. "Ay, Lord!"

Before long they went to bed. The young Wheeler, who was to be one of the several to whom this story will belong, was kept awake awhile by his parents', particularly his mother's, uncertainty that had suddenly filled, more perfectly than light and warmth, the room where they had sat. So far, Wheeler knew this only as a feeling that had returned often enough to become familiar. It was not yet a thought that he could think in words. A day eventually would come when he could think in words of his parents' long worry about money and of the way it afflicted especially his mother. Perhaps because she had been thirteen years old when her mother died, any uncertainty that came to her foreshadowed the worst she could imagine. What is to come? But she knew, and for her this was a worded thought, that farming—the land, the farmers, the farm hands, the animals, and the crops—was the foundation of the nation's economy, where it was also at the bottom of the nation's consciousness and regard, and so would be paid least. She knew where in the order of things her family was and where, she thought, they were destined to be. So far as he then knew these things, Wheeler knew them in his mother's words.

But then Wheeler thought of the journey to Louisville that his father would make the next day. He knew his father would be leaving way in the night, in the dark. He imagined the dark. He imagined his father astride his tall sorrel horse, Sunfish, starting out for Louisville in the dark. When he thought of Sunfish shining in the dark, Wheeler was already sleeping.

He woke to the sound of Sunfish's shod hooves going by the house on the knapped rock of the driveway. Though his father called the horse "Sun" or sometimes "Sunny," Wheeler always called him by his full name, "Sunfish," out of respect, which he gave along with awe and love, because the horse by his presence and bearing

# THE FORCE OF A STORY

seemed to require it. He felt he recognized Sunfish's steps because of their quickness, even in walking, that meant also that his head was up, his eyes wide with watching, and his ears alert. Wheeler listened as the footfalls went on, until perhaps he was only imagining the sound of them. He thought, "It is way in the night. I have never been awake so late in the night. As late as this. Ever before." And again he was sleeping.

His father rode on into the dark. It was a time, familiar in Kentucky winters, when it was cold but thawed, the ground muddy, the sky overcast without rain, the light gray as lead all day, and the nights dark. For a while Marce regretted the need that had taken him out of warmth and sleep and away from home so long before day. So far, he had fended aside the ridiculousness of rising so early to travel so far only to see the last of the crop that had been intimately his work and thought since early March. Now, however, came a moment when it did look ridiculous. Had it not been for his promise to Jim Stedman, Marce might have turned back then and gone home. As he knew, there was nothing more he could do for his crop. Now probably he could only see it sold and accept, as he always had, whatever the buyer wished to pay for it. But there had been agitation among the growers and an effort to organize against the monopoly of James B. Duke's American Tobacco Company. Marce and Mr. Stedman had not taken part, but now they had made up their minds to go and see for themselves if any difference had been made. They were cautious and they were doubtful, but they were going.

Presently Marce yielded himself to his journey. He came into the kind of knowing that the darkness required of him, feeling himself at one with his horse and with the shape of the country that he knew by the tendencies of the road and various looms and shades. His senses had begun their collaboration with Sunfish's. To an extent he could not have defined, he was depending on Sunfish to pick his footing. Though the darkness pressed closely upon them, it was as though he and the horse together were accomplishing a kind of sight. He and Sunfish, whom he trusted now as familiarly as he trusted his own legs, were long past the day when they had reached their understanding. Marce acknowledged compliments on his horse, which came fairly often, by saying, "He'll do."

The horse required governing, and occasional reminding, but he had easy gaits, a long stride, and a willing heart. When necessary, he could get over a lot of ground in a hurry. But Marce, who often hurried

# THE FORCE OF A STORY

himself as a mere reflex of his native eagerness, never asked a work team or a saddle horse for more haste than was necessary. He liked to feel in them a large reserve of strength. Though he seldom urged them out of a walk, he ceaselessly urged them. He liked them to move with their heads up, wide-awake, striding rapidly and long.

He liked as well the strength and endurance he knew in himself, his wakefulness now to the dark and the cold and the country he felt around him, wide open to the sky.

Ahead of him, just as the road began its descent off the ridge into the river valley, he heard a horse nicker. Sunfish answered. And presently out of the dark: "Marce?"

"*Yes*sir, Mr. Jim. How're you this fine morning?"

"I've not called it morning, my boy, but I'm all right."

Jim Stedman had met him at the end of Stedman Lane, true to their plan. This would not be by far the first of their journeys together. In that year, Marce was forty-three, Jim Stedman twenty-five years older. He had been, from Marce's boyhood, the neighbor, the older friend and teacher, that a hard-headed boy needs as recourse from his father—as, in fact, an ally of his father.

## MARCE CATLETT

Mr. Jim or Mr. Stedman, as Marce variously called him, was by then a work-wise elder who farmed well and thriftily what he called his one-man, two-mule farm—a hundred and fifty acres, more sloping than level, much of it wooded. He said little, thought a lot, watched, listened, and was unsurprised, perhaps by then unsurprisable. You had to know him a while before you recognized the fierceness of his independence, for he did not boast of his principles. But though he exchanged work customarily with his neighbors, he had never paid a cent to a hired hand. Marce, whose farm was somewhat larger and laid better, needed the help of a black man, Link DeMint, and his family. This was a difference between Marce and Jim Stedman that they had always taken as a matter of course and did not discuss, though Marce knew that it made his friend a freer man than he was. Mr. Stedman went his way, decently self-reliant, always busy, never hurried. He was a man rarely seen sitting down. A good livestockman, he was not the horseman or teamster that Marce had been since his head more or less had leveled at about the age of twenty-five. His step into that precedence, which Mr. Stedman had acknowledged readily and even with pride, had been Marce's coming of age.

# THE FORCE OF A STORY

Mr. Stedman turned his horse into the dark road a few steps behind, leaving Marce and Sunfish to find the way and set the pace. From time to time, Marce would divert his attention from Sunfish and the way ahead to the footfalls of Mr. Stedman's horse coming steadily on behind him, and he took from the older man's company a pleasure that was a comfort and had become his habit.

As Mr. Stedman was carefully aware, riding in the dark was ordinary for Marce, who, to deal with neighbors or creditors, often would go at night so as to avoid the tollgates. He could not spare the toll, even when he had it, and he knew that every penny saved gave a necessary comfort to Dorie, who lived in fear of subtraction.

As it went down alongside the stream, the road was steep and crooked, but it was graveled, audible and familiar under the shod hooves of their horses. The slopes upward and downward at the sides of the road were wooded and much steeper, and so the descent offered little difficulty to the seeing creature that Marce and his horse had become.

Once they had come down onto the river bottom, the road became more elusive, in places merely a pair of worn tracks. In the dark there was the danger that Sunfish might stray into fencewire, which could make serious trouble in a hurry. But Marce always rode with a peeled stick cut from an elm. He carried it primarily because if Sunfish knew of its presence, he would never need to feel it, but now Marce was using it as a probe to locate the fences in the dark. When one was close, he tapped the top wire steadily to alert the horses. At intervals there were mudholes where drains from the valleyside crossed the bottomland. Marce allowed Sunfish some choice in dealing with the mudholes, places displeasing to both horse and rider, where a horse could sometimes pull off a shoe. But the pressing danger in those places was that in avoiding a mudhole or the worst of it, the horse would sidle out into a fence.

Standing water in the mudholes was lighter than the ground. The tops of the trees along the road were darker than the sky. Almost invariably when they passed a house, barking dogs would tell them where they were. When they went by Aug Palmer's house, a lighted window told them that Aug's wife was still alive and still sick. Finally they saw lantern light shining in the wide-open doorway of a barn. This was at Milt Hardaway's place, where he kept a part-time livery stable for people needing to leave their horses and walk to Eagleville across the railroad bridge. Milt Hardaway was expecting them.

"I allowed you all would get here *about* now," he said. And he helped them to care for their horses. They

# THE FORCE OF A STORY

stabled the horses and fed them, and held out their money to Milt.

"Now you fellows needn't to pay me till you owe me."

"You better take it while we got it," Marce told him.

"Well, you fellows are headed to Louisville, I know," Milt said, and he took their money.

He lit a second lantern, which was part of the deal. And now Mr. Stedman went ahead, carrying the lantern, as they followed the path through a strip of woods between the road and the railroad.

So in their memories the way went: a passage through the dark, undertaken familiarly by men of their kind in their time. So Marce remembered it to Wheeler, who told it to Andy, who in a world radically changed needed a long time and great care to imagine what he heard, but as he has imagined it he has passed it on to his children, for the story has been, as it is still, a force and a light in their place.

Because of the story, there were some kinds of a man that Wheeler could not be, a certain kind that he had to become, and certain things that he had to do. Andy and his children have been similarly limited and prompted by this story. Because they have lived within its terrestrial bounds and reach, they have borne it demandingly in mind. It is still a passage through the dark, revealed to its followers only by love for those they follow, for one another, and by the daylight as it comes.

In the station at Eagleville, Mr. Stedman left the lantern with the stationmaster, to be carried back to Milt Hardaway on their return, and they paid for their tickets. They stood by the stove then with their hands opened to it, merely waiting, until they heard the train wail as it descended into the river valley, and then, the only passengers, they went and stood at the door, looking out. They went out again into the cold as the great engine hove over them, going by with the sounds of a ringing bell, escaping steam, and steel rolling on steel.

They stepped aboard, the conductor waved his lantern, and the train was again moving. They took seats in a dimly lighted car as the clicking of the wheels over the rail joints sped up beneath them. And here the strangeness of their journey began. It was the strangeness of effortless movement. Aside from so rare an event as this on the railroad or the river, neither of them had ever moved but by bodily effort, their own or that of a horse or mule. For them, to be carried passively and swiftly through the dark on the unvarying rails was an experience that required their attention, though they had little speech for it, and though, had they been accustomed to it, they might have slept. They felt in their flesh the ruled line by which the railroad had pierced the living country, subduing its ancient contours to levels and slants and bends required by the machines that ever after would hurry regardlessly across it.

And they themselves for that while were borne by the demand that had sent the rails across the country to bear out of it the work of the hands of such men as themselves, a myriad, from sea to sea. After a time that seemed to them too short, when they had stepped down onto the unmoving pavement, they felt slow and awkwardly balanced on their feet. It was a long walk to the warehouse where their hogsheads of tobacco were stored and would be sold, but they had plenty of time and they knew the way. While they were in the vicinity of the station, though it was still dark, they could feel the city beginning to change from the life in it that continued through the night to the daytime life that began anew every morning. With some frequency they were met or overtaken and passed by wagons drawn by horses trotting at a settled, all-day gait, the hoofbeats resounding in the hollows of the dark streets. Their own steps carried them eastward to where the city performed the fundamental work of joining itself to the country, receiving its produce to be transformed into its own sustenance and that of other cities. This was the district containing the stockyards, slaughterhouses, warehouses, workshops and factories, wharves and railyards. Here their work would pass from the risk, the weather, and the travail of their lives into the possession of a few men elsewhere, whose interest in it would be with fair certainty defended and rewarded. This was a place of handwork and handworkers; of lifting, loading, and hauling; of firing and forging; of weighing and paying.

They were surrounded now by the work of city workers, people not capably poor and self-sustaining, as Marce was, but passively poor, as he felt he could see by their posture and demeanor, a dulled acceptance in their way of moving about their tasks. He could imagine himself doing their work; he could not imagine their lives. His last year's crop, every leaf handled and appraised, pressed into the hogsheads in a layered order that he thought beautiful, he felt now to be disappearing from him. He and Mr. Stedman had become strangers among strangers. He thought he had come too far from home.

They were hungry. In a while they came to an eating place, a plain large room with a bar and tables, where they got an ample workman's breakfast that they

# THE FORCE OF A STORY

could afford. When they came out, the streets had filled with the gray light of the sky.

Under the skylighted roof of the warehouse, the hogsheads of tobacco were lined up, row upon row, each now with a stave broached to display the contents. Among the farmers standing about, singly or in twos or threes, there was little talk. They had not much that they wanted to hear themselves say. Word had got about that they had little to nothing to expect. They had feared so. Soon they were going to know so.

In the quiet of that place, Marce and Mr. Stedman became quiet. When they had come to their own hogsheads, counted and examined them, Mr. Stedman stopped and stood, accepting the wait they had ahead of them, and simply waiting. His ability to wait was what made him, when he wanted a mess of fish, a good fisherman. He could drop his baited hook into the water and then wait, watching the cork, hardly moving, until he did or did not catch a fish.

Marce was never a fisherman. And now he suffered the wait. He walked from one of his hogsheads to another, assuring and reassuring himself of the quality of his crop and of his handling. He had done the best he could, which he knew was better than good enough, and now it was time for the other fellow to step up and buy the crop and the work at a fair price. Now and again he had allowed himself to imagine what it would be to receive a fair price, a decent price, though he feared that he knew better, and he never spoke of such a thing aloud.

In the so-called auction, when it finally began, there was a single bidder. This was the buyer for the American Tobacco Company. Hardly raising his voice, this man bought the hogsheads of tobacco rapidly, one after another, at a few pennies a pound. The great room's cold light became solemnized by a palpable hopelessness. Among the farmers every man had withdrawn his gaze as if into his own heart. Although, like everybody else, Marce had learned what to expect, the single numerals bluntly and forever penciled onto the paper he felt as a wound. There would be no fair payment for him to pick up at the office counter and carry home. As he saw readily enough, the crop would barely pay its way to the market and the commission on its sale. Its purchase, properly named, was theft. He had been robbed of his crop and his work in perfect disregard of broad daylight and of his own presence and eyesight, and he felt the insult.

What came into him then was something he wanted to say, something he would not intend to say until he had heard himself say it. It would be a challenge. By such challenges, thrown out ahead of thought, he had

# THE FORCE OF A STORY

acquired, without intending or much caring, the reputation of a fighter, one who would fight all day if all day was what it took.

Andy Catlett, to whom this story may belong a while longer in its passage through the world, remembers a day when one of the oldest friends of the neighborhood and one of the best, Dr. Stratton, with his left arm disappeared up to the shoulder in the hind end of a cow, said, as he often said, "I may have told you this before. If I have, stop me." And Andy, as always, did not stop him. They had been speaking of Andy's grandpa, Marce Catlett, whom Dr. Stratton remembered well. Dr. Stratton, as he grew older, became more and more dependent on the company of older men of the Social Security cohort, whom he needed only for their company and conversation. One of these had been Iry McConothy.

"Iry McConothy told me he and your grandpa fought all one morning up and down the driveway there in front of the house, with your grandma standing on the porch begging them to stop."

"What were they fighting about?"

"Iry never said."

## MARCE CATLETT

"Well, who won?"

"According to Iry, your grandpa did."

Marce had reared up in a posture that made him conspicuous, and several people were looking at him. But he, as through a pinhole, was seeing only the face of the buyer who continued reciting the predestined small numbers.

What Marce was getting ready to say was just about to be said when he felt a hand on his shoulder. It was a calm and calming touch that he recognized. His vision widened, and instead of the stolid buyer, he was looking at Mr. Stedman, who was standing by him, looking at him. Mr. Stedman shook his head, just a sideward twitch that may have been visible only to Marce, who knew it well and understood it. He had been a mouthy boy and young man, as he still was a reckless one. His friend's precaution had saved him often enough from embarrassing himself, or embarrassing them both. Now Mr. Stedman feared that, in his helplessness, Marce would cry out or lash out, which would only add to his defeat and humiliation. He was telling him, as he had told him many times before, *Don't say a word.*

Mr. Stedman saw that he would be obeyed. But he

# THE FORCE OF A STORY

saw too how tightly Marce had needed to shut his mouth. He was seeing Marce now from the vantage of his own solvency and safety. His place had been paid for long ago, his children were grown, he was on the downslope of his life. But Marce had begun in a hard time his effort to own his farm, he badly needed the money he had just failed to get, his wife feared their ruin, his boys were young. He had a hard pull ahead of him.

Jim Stedman then felt in his heart one of the hardest of human sufferings: the wish to help his friend more than he knew he could. He leaned and took hold of Marce's forearm above the clenched fist and gripped it. He said, barely aloud, "Let's go."

It was only after they had resumed their own force and direction, leaving the station at Eagleville and starting their walk back to Milt Hardaway's barn, carrying the lantern unlit in midafternoon, that Marce was rid of the dullness of having been where he did not belong, and he walked back into his own flesh and consciousness. And it was not until he had again straddled the good horse Sunfish, who bore him eagerly homeward through the gray light and the wind, that he felt himself to be fully the man who had dismounted at Hardaway's in the dark of the morning. He was that man, now changed to the extent of knowing, in dollars lost and dollars owed, more of the cost of the life he now continued to live, so exactingly changed, and yet the very man. For he felt his strength. He felt pressing upward under his heart, under his breath, the force of his willingness to bear his wound and to keep at his work.

He was hungry, for they had eaten nothing since their breakfast. They had left the warehouse knowing, with no need to say, that they could not afford the price of another meal. But hungry as he was, Marce was feeling good. He was feeling defiantly good. And he felt also, like a hunger, his need to get home. He needed to get back from that day's defeat, as completed as it now was, and take up his work again. He had been defeated, but he was not destroyed. He was not, as he knew Jim Stedman was not, dependent solely on the sale of his tobacco. The two of them farmed, to the extent they were able, under the rule of diversity. "If there's a market for it, and you can grow it, and you don't grow it," Mr. Stedman liked to say, "that is a *loss*." The Catletts, like the Stedmans, tried to have something to sell every week, if it was nothing but a basket of eggs. But they had their cattle, their sheep, their hogs. They grew the corn needed by their stock. The tobacco ground and the corn ground of the years before would be covered before frost by the new growth of wheat. Above all, they had from their land and their heritage the means to feed themselves. This was their subsistence, their household economy, that would carry them through that hard time, and again through the hard times still to come. They had also their cooking and heating fuel that they took from their woodlands at the cost only of their work. Conventional economists would price their subsistence at what they could have sold it for, but a true accounting would price it at what it would have cost them to buy it—a crucial difference. If Marce was going home with nothing from that day's sale, he was not going home *to* nothing. He was going home, his thoughts were telling him, to survive, to live, to take up again the work of a tobacco crop for the coming year.

Like most farmers throughout the history of farming, Marce was constrained to farm because it was the only work he knew, though he also had been called to it by his love for it. And this was one of the "resources" that the corporate economy proposed to grow and thrive upon. And the farmers of that kind would return from defeat to work again until they were used up, dead and buried, to be replaced by chemicals and machines, and by farmers of another kind, who borrowed and spent until they too by now are nearly all exhausted, defeated, and gone.

Their return home from Hardaway's barn was far more assured and faster also than their travel over the same distance that morning in the dark. Now they saw the road and chose their way.

At Stedman Lane, they parted company. "Long day," Marce said, lifting his hand.

Mr. Stedman, already turning away, raised his own hand without looking back. "Yep. Was a long 'un."

The ride up from Hardaway's had restored Marce to himself. In his own life and strength and in his soul, he was all right. But now as he rode on alone, he looked ahead to what came next. Though he could find in himself the strength and the willingness that the coming year would demand, it still was true that he would need, and Dorie and the boys would need, the money he had not received. They needed, simply, an economic confidence that they did not have. He knew that Dorie needed, and he needed for her, a little margin of ease, a little letup, in which she could buy for the boys or for herself some pleasing thing that she merely wanted. Beyond his dread of bringing home bad news, he feared, with a fear that had come to be with him always, his failure somehow to head off Dorie's disheartedness, her inability to enjoy any good thing just because it was good and was available. Though she recognized the goodness of the numerous things that satisfied him or made him happy, she saw them passing away. So Marce feared, and so he grieved. And so Wheeler would one day come to speak with power, and to the benefit of his parents and many like them, of a time when his people had not enough of anything except fear.

It was hard for Wheeler to think that such a horse as Sunfish and such a rider as his father could come home with bad news. He and Andrew were in the kitchen with their mother, waiting. It was time, she thought, for Marce to be getting home. They were waiting to eat supper, hoping he would soon arrive. A lamp stood, lighted, in the middle of the table. Though some daylight still remained outdoors, only the lamplight shone in the windows.

They heard Sunfish's hoofbeats on the driveway, going past the house and on across the barn lot to the barn. They waited while, as they almost could see,

Marce unsaddled and brushed the horse, led him to the trough to drink and then to his stall, gave him his ration of corn and hay. They knew even that Marce lingered a moment in the barn door, to assure himself by the sounds that Sunfish was eagerly eating his corn, before he started on to the house. And then they heard his steps on the boards of the back porch, and then his hand on the knob of the kitchen door.

Marce came in and, reaching backward with one hand, pulled the door soundlessly shut. He stood there as soundlessly himself for a long moment, needing to accustom himself again to speech, having said for several hours only his two parting words to Jim Stedman. From the time they had left the warehouse, they had been too much of one mind to need to talk.

He stood, in Wheeler's memory of him, as straight up as Adam must have stood when his strength first exceeded his weight. And Wheeler heard first the silence and then the suppressed fear in his mother's voice.

"Well, Marce, what did it bring?"

"It brought," he said, "nothing."

He unbuttoned his coat, took it off, hung it and then his cap on their nail beside the door, and looked at them again.

He said, "It brought just a little short of what it cost to sell it."

# THE FORCE OF A STORY

It was his mother's silence that Wheeler was hearing then, for she had not replied.

"It paid the railroad, it paid something of the warehouse, nothing to me," his father said.

And Wheeler understood that no more was going to be said about the sale of their crop.

His father said as if in answer, as it seemed to Wheeler, to what his mother had not said, "Dorie, it'll be all right. I'll do what it takes to make it all right."

Wheeler would remember the fear in his mother's silence. He would remember it as the silence of justice outraged and hopeless. But on that night he was able to know only that she meant her silence to conceal her suffering. He felt his breath suddenly shortened by the wish to protect his mother. He wanted more than anything, and this he may have caught from the wish in his father's voice, to help her. If he knew of anything to do that he could do to help her, he would do it.

His father said, still addressing their mother, but now smiling in greeting to her boys, "Mother, could you scrape up a bite to feed a hungry man? My belly thinks my throat's been cut."

The boys laughed then, as they always did when he told them the thoughts and opinions of his belly.

# The Future

# I.

HAVING LONG OUTLIVED ITS ECONOMIC OCCASION—for tobacco, a proven cause of cancer, is now not much grown anymore in its old region—the story lives on in its suffering and sorrow, and as a fragment of the history of humankind's unwillingness to pay farmers for their work or the land for its yield. For those who still remember it, it bears with it still a particular love, and it lives in their hearts and thoughts as a motive to correct a profound and worsening national flaw.

Like Wheeler his father, Andy Catlett has remembered the story as an event central to his life, though it happened nearly thirty years before he was born.

## MARCE CATLETT

Wheeler remembered all the events of the sale of his family's 1906 tobacco crop, from his parents' cautious hope for a sufficient payment of money to his father's return home at nightfall with nothing but a big appetite for his supper. Wheeler remembered as a child remembers, a series of pictures, exactly detailed, accompanied by feelings deeply impressed in his heart, to which the worded story would come as he grew in understanding. He told it to himself surely many times, and to others who needed to hear it. He told it to his children, who told it to their children. And thus the story has so far survived in living memory.

Wheeler kept it in his thoughts and in his heart until the time came when he did know something that could be done to help people like his parents and the two or three farming generations following theirs. He and others who remembered made, with limited help from the federal government, an organization of farmers that for the six decades of its political life gave them an asking price for their tobacco crops. This organization, the Burley Tobacco Growers Co-operative Association, or "the program," as it was called, employed the principles of fair pricing balanced and protected by limiting production to the quantity expectably needed by the manufacturers. Every farm that grew the crop, which about all of them did, was assigned an allotment

# THE FORCE OF A STORY

in keeping with its production in previous years. Its allotment, measured first in acres and later in pounds, would then be marketed at prices set by the program. To the end of his life, Wheeler believed, rightly, that those principles would work for any farm product. All that was needed would be the public will to give farmers and farming a secure place in the nation's economy. That possibility was fading from public consciousness in Wheeler's final years. It will not come again in any future now foreseeable.

Andy Catlett has grown now into the old age of a grandson, son, father, and grandfather. He feels still living in himself the passion by which his grandfather survived the story of his defeat by the Duke monopoly, and the passion with which his father remembered it, and so the passion with which he himself has remembered it and handed it on, so that in his own final years he sees it living still as memory and motive in his children and grandchildren.

The story and the love borne in it, passing down, has held them together like a living root of the same tree, and like a tuned string, across a hundred and eighteen years and five generations. But from the year of our Lord 2025, looking back, Andy sees how breakable, how threatened, how perilously stretched across departures and returns that vital strand has always been.

## MARCE CATLETT

The story of a family at home is like a puzzle put together. Put together, the separate parts cohere in a kind of sense, not otherwise ever to be made: the story of the family at one for a time with the story of its place. The Catlett family cohered in this way until Wheeler went away to college at the age of eighteen. They were until then a family of three—Marce, Dorie, and Wheeler, the elder son, Andrew, having never been very willingly a part of it after he took command of his own legs.

As he grew from boyhood into the strength of a young man, Wheeler learned at his father's side the place, the farm, the round of its yearly work, and he liked it. The family puzzle put together in its place, kept in place long enough, offers to a person's love the possibility of translating itself into work. Wheeler grew into the love of farming. He loved the days he worked to the end of, and from there looked back at the difference he had made. On Sundays he went with his mother to the Bird's Branch church in the morning and attended to his schoolwork in the afternoon. His father met his own sense of religious obligation by a studied deference to a deity perhaps biblical he called the Old Marster.

# THE FORCE OF A STORY

At college Wheeler excelled and gained somewhat the independent use of his mind, but he did not forget where he had come from. Because he had a good mind and liked the use of it, Wheeler was at first a bright and then, in college, a brilliant student. Confidence came to him, and a certain courage, and something in the way of poise. In his senior year he was president of the student body. He was conducting a meeting of the students, gathered into the chapel, when the president of the college stood up to interfere. Wheeler, who knew the rules of order, ruled him out of order. The president, who knew the rules of order, sat down.

Wheeler might have gone from college on out into the world and a good city job or a profession, as many of his generation were doing. But he came home—back, you might say, into the living and ongoing story of his family's endurance in their place. For he had come through his four years of study, his student friendships, even love, as he had thought it, for an attractive girl, with farming and his home farm on his mind. He came home to farm.

He came home also against the current of the time and against the current that had as often set against farmers. A decade before the trouble that would be remembered as "the Depression," the farm economy was already depressed. The farm and their work barely provided two livelihoods, one for Wheeler, one for his parents. Wheeler knew he was cramped, and he knew nothing to do about it.

The history and the presence of hard times for farmers, the continuing vulnerability of the market for tobacco, sporadic agitation among the growers, help from a wealthy newspaper publisher in Louisville, instruction and advice from people experienced in farmer organizations—the convergence of so many causes had started the Burley Tobacco Growers Co-operative Association. When he was out of college and again living at home, Wheeler began to take part in gathering support for this organization. He got into it, as he said, "with both feet." He had known the reasons for it before he could put them into words, and now he spoke the reasons in conversations with his neighbors and in speeches given to meetings in schoolhouses and at picnics. He took part in pageants on the history of tobacco. He farmed and he thought. He talked at every opportunity. He spoke as one thoroughly committed and prepared, and with the passion that had grown in him from the night he had realized his parents' helplessness

# THE FORCE OF A STORY

against the American Tobacco Company of James Buchanan Duke.

And then a great change came to him that he could not have expected, for it came from far outside the light and consciousness of any day he had ever lived.

# II.

AN AMBITIOUS LAWYER AND FRIEND OF THE program, Thomas Franklin, was a candidate in that district for the U.S. House of Representatives. He came one summer night to Port William and delivered his campaign speech from the porch of the hotel. Wheeler, who had worked a long day, did not get to town in time to hear Mr. Franklin. He got there just at the end of Mr. Franklin's speech, while the crowd was still gathered. Many of the crowd knew Wheeler, knew of his efforts for the program, and were proud of his graduation from college, a rare thing in the Port William neighborhood in those days. An old man's voice called out to him: "*You* talk to us, Wheeler boy!" Another voice cried, "Yeah!" A few hands clapped, and then more, and then all. Wheeler stepped up and stood alone on the hotel porch. The crowd faced him and grew quiet.

Wheeler had several advantages that night. He was speaking to his neighbors, who had asked him to speak; he knew what he needed to say; and, because he was at home with his hearers, he knew how to say it. He spoke of the program. He said how he welcomed it. To show the need for it, he told the story of his family's loss and trouble in 1907, a story that belonged to them all and that many of them had lived and remembered. It was the old story, he said, as old as the Bible, of people with too much wealth, too much power, and too little conscience. He quoted old Crawford Horne, a political hero of that region in a time a little earlier: "If you let the corporations rule, the poor man won't have cat guts for fiddle strings nor wood ashes for lye soap." Wheeler's speech was a living strand between him and his hearers. He spoke well. Though he had not heard Mr. Franklin's speech, Mr. Franklin, who had lingered in the crowd, heard Wheeler's.

On that night of their convergence in Port William, the two of them did not meet. But after a few days a letter came to Wheeler from Mr. Franklin: "It looks like I am going to win my race. If I go to Washington, I will need a secretary. Will you go with me?" This question came to Wheeler as a sudden enlargement, as of the sky

# THE FORCE OF A STORY

above his head or his allotment of breath. He became just as suddenly more careful than before in his thoughts about himself and his prospects.

He knew that he had been at a dead end. As things stood, and with the means then available to him, he could not expect to prosper as a farmer. He thought, and the years that followed proved him right, that the outlook was not soon going to improve. But now he had been surprised by an opportunity to look elsewhere. And he looked with all the intelligence he had. If there had been times at school with his friends when he could be frivolous or giddy, all that was behind him now. By the time of Mr. Franklin's letter, he knew himself and his abilities as well probably as he could have done at his age. If now he could look beyond his present circumstances at the possibility of living in Washington as secretary to a congressman, no doubt he felt obliged to look beyond that as well. He could not have regarded employment by Mr. Franklin as a vocation or a life's work, as he once had regarded farming. Marce Catlett was something of a trader, and so was Wheeler. He wrote back to Mr. Franklin: "I am fully aware of the honor you have given me by asking me to assist you in Washington as your secretary. I will be further honored to do so, if you will allow me at the same time to attend law school at night."

It is easy to imagine that Tom Franklin looked upon

Wheeler's terms with some amusement: *The boy is biting off more than he can chew. But let him try.* Wheeler received Mr. Franklin's consent by return mail: "All right. As soon as you need to hear from me again, you will."

Mr. Franklin won his race. When the time came, Wheeler packed his clothes, not many, and took the train to Washington.

At this point in his father's story, old Andy feels his thoughts turn home. He feels how much of what actually was to be the future his father had put at stake and at risk by going away. The once-put-together puzzle of three parts in place was now missing its necessary third part, far away and with no assured return.

If Mr. Franklin had in fact supposed that Wheeler could not chew as much as he had bitten off, he was wrong. By day Wheeler served as Mr. Franklin's secretary—as what now would be a congressman's staff—keeping him caught up in his work in the Capitol, keeping him in touch with his constituents at home, answering the telephone, answering the mail, fending off distractions, and making necessarily his own acquaintance with the offices and some of the officers of the government. At night he attended classes, and he studied.

## THE FORCE OF A STORY

Wheeler's later involvement in the economics and politics of tobacco and his work for the program would have a public, and therefore a historical, importance. But a problem that Wheeler left behind for Andy, and other inquirers, is his evident indifference to his own historical value. His attention, ability, and effort were given unstintingly to dealing with the problems and difficulties that confronted him, *as* they confronted him. Once those were dealt with, there would be others, and he continued his work. That he worked well is sufficiently evident. He prided himself in working well, as is verified by the results, and his speeches that were published are clear, fully formed, and eloquent. Of the personal circumstances in which he worked, and of his thoughts about his work as he was doing it, he said little and wrote nothing. He filed his correspondence, of course, but he kept nothing in the way of a journal, and Andy doubts that he ever considered doing so.

As a result, Andy knows too little of his father's Washington years. He knows that, among his other duties, his father had to take care that Mr. Franklin did not embarrass himself by becoming drunk in public. Of this he heard his father speak only once, and then, in loyalty, he used a metaphor: "I would see that he had torn his pants, and I would need to get to him." From a number of things overheard or heard in passing, Andy knows that his father worked extremely hard during those years. He told Andy once that he had sometimes gone for days without sleeping. Andy guesses from what he knows of himself that his father may have dozed for brief spells over his book or his writing paper during the long, wakeful nights, or he may have fallen into naps that seemed afterward to have been only blinkings of his eyes. It is nonetheless easy for Andy to imagine that there were stretches of several days when his father did not go to bed.

For Andy does know how well and thoroughly his father studied, and this he knows from evidence that is plentiful enough. The only relics of Wheeler's Washington years that seem to have mattered to him are a textbook, *Cases on Constitutional Law*, and a stack, as tall as wide, of pages mostly handwritten, tied with a string. The textbook was 1,404 pages, and virtually all of those that Andy has turned bear Wheeler's careful annotations in pencil. On the stack of pages, his father seems to have briefed or analyzed every case that he encountered in his studies. His annotations in the book and his written summaries have the character not of notes made in preparation for tests, but rather of a relentless self-testing. He seems to have denied himself any willingness to pass through his reading without understanding

# THE FORCE OF A STORY

thoroughly what he had read. On all those hundreds of pages his sentences are swiftly written—the crosses of the *t*'s flying above the lines of script—but nonetheless careful, economical, and complete. The style is direct, the syntax strong. He was in search of the essential points of contested events, of arguments, precedents, and judgments. He seems to have thought—rightly, his son thinks—that what he knew was tested and secured by his ability to write it into sentences. Using only the necessary technical or legal terms, he wrote with practiced elegance in plain English, the common tongue, as if speaking to a jury of his neighbors. He had already formed his lifelong habit of speaking clearly and for clarification, as well as his settled conviction of the need to "study your lessons."

Throughout his years in Washington, Wheeler kept to the pace and the standards he had set for himself. Eventually it was recognized by Mr. Franklin, and others, that Wheeler's way of putting himself to work was characteristic, bred in the bone, and not a too-high perch that he was bound to fall from. And so Wheeler became a young man favorably spoken of, followed by appraising looks and high expectations. A day came, by the doing of Mr. Franklin and a colleague, when Wheeler received a truly outstanding job offer from a large meat-packing company in Chicago.

But Wheeler did not appear to be as enthusiastic about the offer as Mr. Franklin had allowed himself to expect. He was treating it merely as something he needed to think about. Mr. Franklin's relationship with Wheeler had so far been good, and they worked comfortably together. Across the difference in their ages, they had become friends. And now Mr. Franklin was reluctant to assume the posture and demeanor of the older man. But on the fourth morning of his own silence about the letter from Chicago, he called Wheeler in and said, "Sit down." Wheeler sat down, and Mr. Franklin turned in his chair so that they were sitting face-to-face. And then Mr. Franklin for some moments sat and thought. As much as he had come to respect Wheeler, and partly because he respected him, he was in some doubt about him. For such a young man as Wheeler, the way between an office in the Capitol and an office somewhat elevated in some great corporation was a beaten track. It was almost a law that had to be obeyed. And yet having observed him closely for three years, Mr. Franklin knew that Wheeler did not fit the usual pattern of the ambitious young man. He clearly was worked upon by ambition of some kind, but the mold that had shaped

# THE FORCE OF A STORY

him was to be found nowhere in Washington. He was, by the usual measures, not predictable, and Mr. Franklin was worried.

He leaned forward and planted a stiffened forefinger on Wheeler's knee. He told Wheeler more plainly than before how much he thought of him. He told him how highly he rated his abilities. He told him how highly he was ranked among his peers by the offer from Chicago. He said, "Wheeler, listen. Don't, damn it, throw this opportunity away."

"Thank you, Mr. Franklin," Wheeler said. "I understand. I'll think about it."

Long ago as that was, Andy's old heart now does surely tremble for his young father as he imagines him leaving Mr. Franklin's office with so great a burden upon him. "Oh, stand by him," he prays. "Let him come home."

Andy never before has prayed or heard of so displacing a prayer, which sets him outside such sense as he so far has been able to make, outside even of time and into the great outside, the eternity maybe it is, that contains time. He seems to have spoken not from his own heart only, but from the hearts also of his grandma and grandpa, his mother, his wife, his children, his grandchildren, and others, many others, or he is praying their prayers as they stand with him in that boundless outside. It is a prayer also for his home country and his home history. For if Wheeler had gone away to make his life in Chicago, an incalculable difference would have descended into his absence. Many lives that have been lived and are being lived could not have been, and many yet to be lived could not be. In Wheeler's absence, the story of his family's loss and suffering in 1907, so strong a memory and motive as it has been in his mind, and in other minds following his, would not have been told again to anybody to whom it would have mattered, if he ever told it again—the story that, at home, would call him into a service that nobody else could have performed as he performed it. Andy cannot fathom the sense or the scope of his prayer. He can only pray it. "Oh, stand by him. Let him come home."

But Wheeler's need to "think about it" was shortcut by an inspiration that came to him as if in answer to the prayer that his elderly son would pray a century later. This part of his story Wheeler enjoyed telling, and often told.

Sitting in his own office subjoined to Mr. Franklin's, he let himself be still and drew the quiet around him. And then a question came to him: *Do I want to spend my*

# THE FORCE OF A STORY

*life looking out a window at tarred roofs, or do I want to see bluegrass pastures?*

He stood up. He went back into Mr. Franklin's office. He said, "Mr. Franklin, I'm going home."

Mr. Franklin said, "WHAT?"

# III.

THEY REMAINED FRIENDS, EVER DEARER TO EACH other as time went on. The ten years between their ages became a smaller difference as they grew older and had in common more experience and more memories. After Wheeler had come home and started his law practice, when Mr. Franklin ran again for his seat in the House of Representatives, he asked Wheeler to be his campaign manager, and Wheeler managed every one of his campaigns after that. In the years before Wheeler married, when he still lived at home with his parents, Mr. Franklin would often spend a night or two in the "company room." He entered into a kind of sonship to Marce Catlett, listening closely to him as he spoke of the history he had lived and of what he had learned. Later, talking to Andy,

## MARCE CATLETT

Wheeler remembered a night when he and Mr. Franklin returned to the home place close to midnight after a distant meeting. As they were leaving the car, a pack of hounds drove a fox along the fence at the back of the barn. To Andy, this way of landmarking an event of his public life is profoundly characteristic of his father.

Through the twenties and the thirties the effort to sustain the tobacco program continued, and after Wheeler returned home he resumed his involvement. His friendship with Mr. Franklin was useful to him then, and in various ways it was useful to the program. It became more useful after the program was reorganized under Roosevelt's New Deal, after Wheeler had become vice president of the program and Mr. Franklin had moved to the Senate. Mr. Franklin became the program's mainstay in Washington, as the program and the good it did became a sort of platform for him in Kentucky. The friendship that had begun with Wheeler's speech in Port William became ten and then twenty and more years old, and much good came of it.

When Marce Catlett died in the winter of 1946, Wheeler received a telegram from Mr. Franklin: "He lived long enough to raise us all."

# IV.

ANDREW CATLETT, WHEELER'S BELOVED OLDER brother, the buddy and boon companion of Andy's childhood, did not submit or in the least subscribe to the motives that had kept the Catlett family continuous and somewhat coherent for the past two or three generations and maybe longer—assuming that he even recognized the existence of those motives or of such motives. He was instead one in the sequence of feral offshoots that fairly regularly had dissented from it. He was not an outcast, because he had never been cast out.

He was never cast out—which his father, on his own, had been of a mind to do—because he was too well loved by his mother, his brother, and everybody else. His advantage, which also was his problem, was that he was a man exceedingly and uniquely attractive. His good looks made him attractive to women, and so no doubt did his way of paying attention to them, which had not been in the least altered or toned down by his marriage at an early age to a woman who had wanted to possess him for the qualities that had put many women into his possession, but who, after she had somehow got him, had no idea on earth what to do with him.

He was perhaps as attractive to men, at least to a certain kind of men, as to women, because of his big laugh and his readiness to do anything anybody else would do.

Andy Catlett, namesake of his uncle Andrew, has now survived his uncle by eighty years. He has lived in the world forty-one years longer than his uncle did. He is certain from what he saw that in the presence of his five-years-younger brother, Andy's father, a man of serious purpose, his uncle Andrew conducted himself with propriety and modesty. But with Andy, who contrived if possible to be with him all day of every day he was not in school, he was not capable of prolonging any sort of deception. Andy knew that Uncle Andrew would say anything he thought. And so he knew, within the limits of his comprehension, the things his uncle thought.

That way of saying whatever he thought got him killed in the summer of 1944, a month and two days before Andy would be ten years old. He was killed with two pistol shots for saying something utterly rank and raw that the man who killed him thought too intimately insulting to be forgiven.

Uncle Andrew has been for Andy a course of study that has continued all his life. In the days and years that followed that life-dividing death, he grew of course into clearer and better knowledge of what he had learned from and about his uncle while he lived. Gradually from the people, his friends, who lived as tenants or hired hands on the two farms once owned and owed-for in partnership by his uncle and his father, he learned things he had had no way of learning for himself.

While his uncle lived, Andy knew nothing of his drinking or his drunkenness. He thinks that nobody knew then, and there is no way of knowing now, whether this was alcoholism or merely an excess belonging to the rowdy nightlife his uncle conducted with his friends—one of whom in his old age delightedly told a friend of Andy's, "We did everything we thought of."

Other friends, Andy's workmates on one of the farms now owned and owed-for only by his father, had seen a part of his uncle's life that Andy heard and soon enough believed but was slow to imagine. When he was too drunk or hungover to function, that unruly man, who had the cleverness merely of his need for secrecy, would conceal his problem by driving his car into one of the barns least likely to be visited or looked into by Andy's father, where he would sleep himself sober.

Over the years Andy has realized, and confessed with some reluctance even to himself, that his beloved Uncle Andrew was "wild" in a sense of that term exclusively human. Unlike the wild animals, so called, Andrew Catlett willingly obeyed no law. He defined himself simply by his impulses and his wants. He was too urgently his own, essentially solitary, self even to be cautious. Maybe he was susceptible to fear, but fear, even fear, informed him of nothing to do that he was not capable of doing. Age and the coming of age—he died at the age of forty-nine—taught him nothing. Between what he thought and what he said, or what he thought and what he did, there was no interval for further thought. Maybe this was an inborn mental or moral vacancy. Whatever it was, it made him an outlaw. When he was shot and killed, having delivered offhand an outrageous insult, he was standing outside any law and all law, where he had as usual placed himself, where he had been standing many years, maybe always.

—

# THE FORCE OF A STORY

And yet, ready as he was to simplify himself, he cannot be easily explained.

Andy was named for him at his request, for he knew that he would have no child of his own.

And eager as Andy was to be with him, that was possible because Uncle Andrew waked him up with a phone call on every workday morning all summer.

The phone would ring in Andy's still-sleeping house. Andy would hurry to pick up the receiver. Uncle Andrew's voice would say, "Come around, baby." Andy, not replying, would hang up the phone, dress, and hurry around to breakfast with Aunt Judith and Uncle Andrew.

And that, Andy supposes after his reckonings of many years, must have given Uncle Andrew something he needed.

# V.

WHEELER CATLETT BOUGHT THE MACK CRAYTON place near the end of the Depression as a part of his plan for sobering and rehabilitating his wayward brother, Andrew. In the summer of 1945, the summer after his uncle Andrew was killed, Andy came to be eleven years old. In that summer, Andy's father's tenant on the Crayton place, the half-rascal Jake Branch, was the first to put Andy to work for wages, the first to send him alone to the tobacco patch, carrying a hoe and a file—"When you can step on the head of your shadow, come in to dinner"—and the first to trust him to work a team of horses by himself, harrowing a field of corn. Jake trusted Andy and put him to work as another member of his family, granting no deference to his youth and allowing him no excuses because he was his father's son. He gave Andy grownup work to do, and a grownup cussing if he did it wrong.

For these accomplishments Andy acknowledges a large debt to Jake Branch. But much of Andy's life in the years following his uncle Andrew's death is overshadowed by questions that Andy could not ask then and cannot answer now. A lot of Andy's upbringing had been given into the care and influence of his uncle. Never mind that his uncle's care and influence had not been as responsible as his father probably thought. Andy anyhow was one of the problems left behind by Uncle Andrew. Andy had entirely loved him, had loved to be with him, partly no doubt because Uncle Andrew demanded so little of him. That Uncle Andrew outranked Andy and was in charge of him was not much of a burden to either of them. And now in the absence of the authority, such as it was, of the man who had been his buddy, and for want of an effective replacement, Andy was in charge of himself, which would hardly do for a boy of ten and then eleven years old. Andy was perhaps not a bad boy, but he was headstrong, full of opinions, judgments, principles of a sort, uncomfortable with himself, resentful of the authority of his parents and teachers, and no doubt disordered by grief for his uncle's death. Andy thought he went to work for Jake Branch because

# THE FORCE OF A STORY

Jake needed him and offered him a job. But must that not have come about actually by the contrivance of his father, who saw that his difficult son needed to be put to work, and needed even more a boss such as Jake was likely to be? Well. That may be a good guess.

Andy's father delivered him every morning to make him one of Jake and Minnie Branch's household, which consisted of his children, her children, their children, Jake's son-in-law Col Oaks, and his live-in hired hand, Leaf Trim. Wheeler called it "Jake's Assortment," all of whom, if they were big enough and not needed for housework, were employed at farmwork.

At noon, if no outsider happened by, there would be fourteen of them around the big table in Minnie's kitchen. The field crew, urged by Jake to "Eat till it's gone" and "Don't ask for nothing you don't see," would help themselves from the bowls and platters of what amounted to a daily banquet, spearing repeatedly with their forks the biscuits that Minnie served piled up in a wash pan. At those meals nothing store-bought came to the table except salt, pepper, the baking powder in the biscuits, and the sugar in the pie. They ate, as the psalmist says, the labor of their hands.

The last thing in the evenings, Andy's father came in his misused automobile to find his son wherever the day's work had taken him, and delivered him to his grandma Catlett's, where he had been living much of the time since his grandpa's death, and almost daily Andy had been enlarged by some knowledge that he knew his father had intended him to acquire, and by some from which he supposed that his father's innocence should be protected.

In those days the Crayton place was a farm intimately inhabited and worked. It was divided into fields known by name, connected by wagon tracks and footpaths. Some of the field boundaries had grown shaggy with trees and bushes where members of Jake's Assortment picked raspberries and blackberries for pies and preserves, or simply picked and ate. Large trees presided over places in the fields where grazing animals shaded in the heat of the day, and where people at work sat a while to rest and talk. The hollows were wooded and inhabited by woodland creatures. At work, early in the summers, they drank freely from wet-weather springs, for the age of poisons had as yet only begun to taint the farmland. There were ponds and a large rock-walled pool where boys could swim or fish. The landmarks served also as mindmarks, for they gathered and held the memories of times and events needing to be remembered.

Eventually, as Andy would live to see, this geography of human memory and amenity would be bulldozed clean away from the mere surface of the ground.

# THE FORCE OF A STORY

What Andy did not understand about Jake's Assortment, in its time and for long afterward, was its prosperity. It was soundly and somewhat exuberantly prosperous. This was owing first to its traditional independence of character and means, along with its traditional subsistence economy, in which by the work of their hands its members fed themselves and their stoves. Had they been poor—and the lords of the tobacco corporations, once upon a time, had scheduled them to be poor—this home economy would have kept them well fed and warm in winter.

"I'll never starve!" Jake would proclaim, one eye winked, the other cocked and glittering. "They may run me out, but they'll never starve me out!" And so he and his household procured a certain wealth from the ground under their feet by means of an inherited wealth in their minds, backs, and hands. They were not going to starve, which meant that past a set limit they would not be poor.

The limit would be set by the availability of land and the duration of a culture, both of which, even so soon, were declining into jeopardy. Back then, the Branches, like every other farm family in that country—like, in fact, both sets of Andy Catlett's grandparents—were practicing a kind of self-sustenance that was an ancient wealth sounder than dollars, taken for granted by themselves, necessary to themselves, but in the times soon to come depreciated almost to extinction, and sometimes into helpless poverty. Like the Branches, like his grandparents, Andy took their way of life for granted. He did not know how old it was or what it was worth or how threated it had come to be. He did not begin consciously to honor and love it until he saw it going away. Finally, in its almost completed absence, he saw it as his native culture: the customs and refined skills of dwelling at home. The doctors of the universities regarded it, and regard it still, as "backwardness," but a culture was what it was, shared and practiced in common by all the kinds and races of the country people, a possession of incalculable worth.

At the time Andy knew them, the Branches, wealthy as they were in their traditional subsistence, were prosperous also in the way of money. This was because of the tobacco program. To the extent that Wheeler Catlett had helped to make and preserve the program, Jake's Assortment was living in the story that began with the calamity of the 1906 tobacco crop, a crop and a calamity that belonged to the Catlett family, the Branch family, and thousands of others.

In its time that story was suffered by nearly everybody on the farms and in the country towns. It was a story that was lived far more numerously than it has been remembered, but a lot of people in Wheeler Catlett's generation remembered it. Because they remembered it, there was an extraordinary mutuality among them. There was a lot that they did not have to explain to one another. It might be argued that this story, so commonly known and understood, was the force that made the Burley Tobacco Growers Co-operative Association. That program was embodied, and for decades maintained, by rememberers like Wheeler, who had witnessed and remembered in their hearts the effects of corporate plunder and indifference.

The story was less remembered in Andy's generation than in his father's, still less in succeeding ones. By now there is no politics and no party that stands for, or would recognize, the indispensable loving care for the farmland and the farm communities that was still prominently voiced in the politics of Wheeler Catlett's generation. And so the story, for the time being at least, has no political life. But it has been remembered continuously in Andy's family so far, perhaps in others, and it has retained so far a formative power.

# MARCE CATLETT

---

For a century and more after the time it happened, the story has been kept in living memory, and so it has had a future. It has been joined to the story of its own survival and influence. If it has at present no public life, it continues to live locally, to inspire local work, and to produce local benefits. So far, it has not ended.

# VI.

WHEN ANDY WAS STILL A SMALL BOY—THAT IS, too small to be useful as a farmhand—his grandma often made a companion of him. He would tag along after her at her work, fascinated at the variety of things she could do, and so learning to do some of them himself. Though he had ridden with her in a horse and buggy through the countryside in search of wild berries to pick, he had never seen her work a mule in the garden. But she did in the garden everything that could be done with a hoe or by hand. She did for her chickens and turkeys all that they required of her. She could milk a cow if she needed to, as Andy discovered to his shame when he neglected his chores. When the milk came to the house from the barn, she strained it into crocks, set the crocks in the cellar to cool, skimmed off the cream when it rose, churned the cream into butter, and shaped the butter into pats of about a pound apiece, which she ornamented by crisscrossing their tops with the edge of the butter paddle.

Watching and listening as she worked, Andy learned something of her mind. It was an old mind, as he would come to understand. It was contemporary insofar as it had acquired the knowledge of younger people, but it was also continuous with minds that had come and gone long before hers. That was because she had not been too much in school. For her generation, formal schooling stopped with the eighth grade, and so the culture that went along with her education was the culture of childhood, which was ages old:

> When I went down by the garden gap
> There I met Dick Red Cap,
> Stem in his hat, stone in his throat,
> Guess me this riddle and I'll give you a groat.

As Andy eventually would know, none of his family had known what a groat was for three hundred years.

Though she owned a radio and would live to own

# THE FORCE OF A STORY

a television set, the telephone was still new to her, and she faithfully covered it with a feather pillow at the start of a thunderstorm, believing that the pillow insulated against lightning that otherwise might follow the telephone wires into the house. As she did this, she invariably quoted Luther Shoals: "I always done that myself, Dorie, until I saw lightning strike a goose." And she counseled Andy in the words of old Uncle Eb Markman: "Never was a man any account that couldn't keep a sharp knife in his pocket." When she heard the first katydid, she said, "It'll be six weeks to frost." She said, "When the oak leaves are big as a squirrel's ear, it's time to plant corn." She said, "A heavy locust bloom means a good corn year." And she knew a prophecy that she repeated on every cold day in the spring: "A time will come when you'll not know the winter from the summer but by the budding of the trees."

From early in his childhood it was plain to Andy that his Catlett grandparents were somewhat in disagreement. There were differences between them that had become sore.

He knew with the same unworded clarity that his grandma was not a happy woman. She loved greatly the things and people she loved, but with a premonition of grief. She saw that the Lord gives good gifts, but the conviction that went straight to her heart was that He gives what He will take away. These thoughts she revealed to Andy, not because of any wish of hers to do so, but simply because she could not help it. Her candor in her old age was what it must have been when she was a child.

She belonged to a kind of world and a kind of life that she was the last of, that Andy would remember as his own determining heritage. It was wearing out as his grandparents' generation wore out, just when it was about to be overtaken by the machine civilization that followed World War II. To Andy, his grandma's kitchen became emblematic of that time in both of their lives. It was a large room, prepared to be busy in a large way. Its focus was an imperious wood-burning cookstove with a firebox at one end and a reservoir for heating water at the other, and two "warming closets" at more or less head-height. The table and high-backed chairs were still a set but old and hard-used. The tabletop swayed in the middle, and the chairs had broken rounds. They bore several coats of paint, in places worn through to the wood, and the wood was polished by handling. The thought of replacing them had never become thinkable. In the pantry, Grandma Catlett kneaded her dough for biscuits and pie crusts on a broken slab of marble that once had been a dresser top. Her kitchen cabinet contained plates, bowls, cups and saucers, and drinking glasses once parts of sets, survivors of generations of breakage. The table knives were black along their cutting edges, where the silver plate had worn off the base metal.

This collection of remnants was completed by a set of habits, old inheritance and familiarity, and a genius native to the circumstances. Without the benefit, so far as Andy knows, of any recipe ever read or written, his grandma was a fine cook. The daily cycle of meals—a big breakfast, a big dinner, a supper of leftovers from dinner—had been all her life the order of her household. Her cooking, invariably good, and Grandpa's appetite, likewise invariable, brought them perhaps as near to mutuality as they ever came.

Their fiftieth wedding anniversary, their Golden Wedding, came in the summer of 1944. Its celebration—delayed a year by the death of their eldest son, Andy's beloved Uncle Andrew, in that summer—was held in the summer of 1945 at Andy's parents' house in Hargrave. It was a moderately large to-do, with dinner in the dining room, the table let out full length. Grandma wore her summer church dress and a hat of lacquered black straw. To Andy's surprise, Grandpa wore a black three-piece suit, a white shirt, and a necktie that appeared to Andy to have been tied by his father. With that finery he wore his only shoes, the high-topped work shoes of the kind that he had worn every day of his life. Andy had never seen the suit, but clearly it had been carefully preserved, as later he would assume, for Grandpa to be buried in, and he did at last wear it to his grave. Two of the children of one of Grandpa's sisters had come all the way from St. Louis to pay their respects, to stay several days at the home place, and to visit the graveyard at Port William. Andy's mother, who was not his grandma's favorite person, was nevertheless careful to do things right. She provided for Grandpa a white carnation for his lapel, and for Grandma a truly beautiful corsage of fragrant yellow roses.

Andy has never been able to imagine clearly enough how his father had gotten Grandpa groomed for the occasion. But he saw, also to his surprise, that Grandpa had submitted with an acceptance that preserved his integrity, and that he responded with graciousness to the guests' greetings and congratulations—which he received, even so, as if on behalf of somebody unknown to them and to him. Of that day Andy chiefly remembers how far it managed to graduate his grandpa from where he belonged. And how his grandpa had managed to graduate himself from the formality of the occasion and the visiting relatives back into his everyday clothes, his place, and his life, Andy has not been able to imagine at all. He himself in his now-long life has made many times the traverse between places he has belonged and places he has not belonged, and it remains to him a change, a difference of being, almost as unimaginable as that between life and death.

His grandpa did not see another summer. He died in February 1946. After that, Andy made pretty much a regular thing of staying with his grandmother, to be company for her and to help her so far as he could to keep to her accustomed ways. At night after supper, while the nights were long, they went into the living room to sit until bedtime. This was when Andy was supposed to do his homework. But his conscience was easily satisfied and his grandma easily deceived. When he had done his work, Grandma would continue her sewing, and they would listen to the radio.

The radio, a small one ordered from a catalog, sat on a nicely embroidered scarf on the top of a small table near the front window. The table had a wide, shallow drawer that Andy did not open in Grandma's presence. But often when he was safely alone he opened the drawer and studied its contents. The drawer contained a haphazard collection of things, accumulated over many years, that nobody knew what to do with: a clay tobacco pipe with a broken stem that Grandpa had plowed up in the garden, a little notebook in which only the first three pages were covered with figures, the remnant of a small four-barreled pistol that a workman had found under the house, a handsome fountain pen that had been dropped on its point. There was a pocket knife, a leather coin purse, about a third of a plug of Days Work chewing tobacco—things Andy did not need to be told were in his grandpa's pockets when he last took off his clothes. He would realize only later that his grandma had saved the cut plug because she was not capable of throwing away anything that had cost money. Tucked against one side of the drawer, carefully separate from the clutter, was the brown, dry, no-longer-touchable, still-fragrant corsage of once-yellow roses.

Though he was then grieving himself over the death of his uncle Andrew, his elderly black friend Dick Watson, and now his grandpa, Andy did not know much about grief. He was young, distracted by his unhappiness in school and his happiness in his life outdoors, his grief muted within him by its wordlessness and by everybody else's inability to think that a boy so troublesome could be grieving. But in the times he spent with his grandmother over several years, he learned of grief by signs that he would understand only later, as his own years and griefs accumulated.

# THE FORCE OF A STORY

His grandma would occasionally tell him some episode of his uncle's characteristic wildness, something that only he would have said or done, and her laughter then she could neither prevent nor approve. But he saw, even so, that grandma's grief for his uncle Andrew was dreadful and permanent. Andy knew that his uncle had been killed. He did not know yet that Uncle Andrew had virtually invited his death by needlessly and in a kind of hilarity insulting the man who killed him. And so Andy eventually would know that his grandmother's grief was not only for her great loss but for the moment when Uncle Andrew might have resisted his confirmed habit of saying anything he thought just because he had thought it. But in Andy's ignorance, when his elders had still been able to shield him from the knowledge that they, anyhow, could not have spoken, he only saw and remembered how his grandma would sometimes sit long in her armchair with her forehead leaning upon her hand. And sometimes he would hear her muttering as she climbed the stairs at bedtime, "Oh, my poor boy. May God have mercy on my poor boy." And he understood that those were her thoughts speaking. To him or to anybody, so far as he was aware, she did not speak of her grief for Uncle Andrew. That, as Andy finally supposes, would have granted too decided a standing to his death and his wildness that yet, even yet, by the mercy of God might be absolved.

Of his grandpa she spoke as thoughts came to mind. His departure weighed upon her as a sorrow, but it also seemed to free her to return to her memories of him when he was young, and she recovered her old delight in him.

One Sunday afternoon he came courting, driving a half-broke good young horse to a buckboard. So eager had he been to present himself that he forgot to tie the horse, who naturally ran off, so damaging the buckboard that the young man, whom Andy knew only as Grandpa, had to go home on horseback.

Several times, as if to summon her vision of him as he had been, Grandma quoted a man whose testimony she obviously treasured: "Marce Catlett is the finest looking man on the back of a horse that ever I saw."

After they were married, she would be at her housework, and she would hear him off in the distance, calling his cattle. His call was beautiful. And she would think, in the style surely of poems remembered from her school readers, "Oh, that such a voice should ever cease!"

And there was the corsage she had put away in the table drawer. Andy is sure it was the only corsage she was ever given or ever wore. Perhaps it stood in her mind

# THE FORCE OF A STORY

for an unpaid tenderness, an uncompletable cherishing. But Andy took from it a knowledge beyond speech. He has at least only his memory, or his seeming memory if that is what it is, of the roses' fragrance emanating from the opened drawer and filling the room.

# VII.

AS HE GREW UP ANDY DID NOT LEARN TO KNOW his grandfather Catlett as a man living to the end of his story, though he heard in passing bits of the story, and he remembered those. What he was most aware of and what he best remembered in the part of his boyhood that remained after his grandfather's death in 1946, was the tone of voice and the way of speaking by which the old man referred, in everything he said, to the story he had lived and what it had taught him. Andy's memory kept precisely also the figure and stance of his grandpa, who with age had bent somewhat forward at the hips, but whose back remained straight as long as he lived—who, though mounting his saddle mare put him to ever greater effort, became visibly younger and entirely capable once he had taken his seat. Seated or standing, his bearing spoke the assurance and readiness of a man who had lived long and ably in a place and in ways intimately loved and known—or, as Andy has come to realize, intimately loved and therefore known, intimately known and therefore loved.

Andy is sorry to remember that as small boys he and his brother sometimes provoked their grandfather to anger and outrage, sometimes innocently and because of their innocence, sometimes because they had learned in their innocence that he could be provoked and they would provoke him deliberately, for the thrill of the risk of his anger. But his term of endearment for each of them was "baby," always tenderly spoken. As evidence gathered around him that he was the last of his kind in that place, Old Marce saw the likelihood—and, as he thought it, the danger—that the childish innocence of his grandsons would grow, and by their other elders would be allowed to grow, into a shameless ignorance of the things most important to him. He never ceased to test their acquirement of knowledge that he considered fundamental: Did they know "gee" from "haw"? Which of a pair of mules was in the "lead," which was on the "off" side? Which was the best of the pair? What fault did they see in the other? Could they see the difference, for that matter, between any two comparable

# THE FORCE OF A STORY

things—between, for instance, a good teamster and a poor one? A good hand and a poor one?

For him, morality began with a moral fear of the waste of daylight, particularly of the morning light. He believed with the passion of old custom and his own long observance that at four o'clock in the morning a man should be awake, on his feet, and at the barn, caring for what needed care, feeding what needed to be fed. Andy remembers coming awake to the feel of his grandpa's stiffened fingers prodding the bedclothes, and the old voice announcing with true grief, "Baby, the sun is shining in your eyes, and you're still laying in the bed!"

Andy came into the world just in time to know his grandfather Catlett in the final decade of his life, and just in time moreover to grow into and to know his grandfather's world in the final decade of its life, before it vanished almost completely, almost at once, after the end of World War II. The war ended in September 1945. Grandpa Catlett died in February 1946. By the crop year of 1950, virtually every farmer was using a tractor.

If Grandpa Catlett's world, from a lunar point of view, was the same as the present world, from the Port William point of view it was a world of an older kind. The life of that former world, within the boundary of Grandpa's farm and the bounds of his neighborhood, was still predominantly the life of creatures. Its work was performed by people and mules or horses, using energy supplied by the light and warmth of the sun. Industrial changes had in fact begun to enter that world years before Andy's birth, but until perhaps his twelfth year—the year following the war—they had come slowly. Until about then, his childhood allowed him to think that his home place had always been and would always be as it then was. He learned it eagerly as it then was, and he loved it. He took it to his heart and aspired to it. In vision then he saw himself as a grown man, a farmer, empowered and entranced by the excellent team of mules his grandpa would have chosen for him to work.

And then in that country, really all of a sudden, the tie was broken between human work and the descent of light from the free and holy sun. That tie to daylight, freely given, a gift as old as creation, was replaced by bondage, purchased by money, to fuels extracted from the darkness under the earth.

# VIII.

AT THE END OF HIS BOYHOOD, HALF A DOZEN years after they parted with all of his grandpa that could die, a time came to Andy Catlett that brought his own mortal being and strength into his mind.

As often in those years, Andy was working as a hired hand for Elton Penn, which involved him as a matter of course in the farming partnership between his father and Elton, who had cooperated in buying one of the first pickup hay balers. The baler belonged to the beginning of the postwar industrialization of farming. It was a heavy, awkward machine that sometimes worked well, sometimes approximately. Sometimes it stood still, waiting upon frantic repairs. To draw the baler, Elton used his large tractor. To rake the hay into windrows and to do some of the mowing, Andy's father had bought the small tractor that began the obsolescence of the mule teams of Grandpa Catlett's time and the times before. Soon they were gone, and with them a grace and a kind of love that farming in that country would not foreseeably know again.

That morning Andy was at work behind the barn where Grandpa Catlett had stabled his horses and mules. He was attaching to his father's tractor one of the earliest tractor-mounted mowing machines. Like the baler, the mower had been designed to work well on a concrete floor or perhaps a football field. It became squeamish and accident-prone when applied to the surface of the actual earth. Attaching the mower to the tractor required alignment of several slots on the framework of the mower with several stud bolts on the tractor, a precision achievable only by "main strength and awkwardness" as Elton said. Only dogged persistence made it possible, and in those summers of the mid-century it had to be done repeatedly, as the tractor would be needed for different kinds of work. Andy had been at it by himself for an hour or more, grateful for the shadow cast by the barn and for the breezes that from time to time cooled the sweat on his face.

He was laboring that morning to fit, so far as he was able, his father's new, fire-driven, labor-saving machine

# THE FORCE OF A STORY

into the nature of that country and into the story of his family's so far uncompleted effort to make itself at home there. Though he did not know it yet, Andy was participating in history. Starting about then, the machines would intrude into history and direct it toward an outcome that Marce and Dorie Catlett, in their order of life, could not have imagined—and that, in fact, their young grandson could not imagine. The machinery would enlarge and complicate itself until not just the mule teams would be gone from the fields, but nearly all the people as well.

In those years of his coming of age, Andy was more simple-minded than he had been before or ever could be afterward. He had loved profoundly his grandpa's way of farming, when people and animals had collaborated in ways long known and now gone, and in a quietness also oldfangled and gone. Later, his mind would become increasingly troubled as the machine-civilization subdued the land and the people to a rule entirely alien to both.

In the years between his childhood and his marriage that finally would make him a grownup, he was something like a technological determinist or a technological fatalist. But those labels flatter him. What he mainly gave his mind to then was an aspiration combining a car and a girl. Such things could be pretty at times, as such things can sometimes be, but those memories have at last become a trial to his patience.

The hot sunlight was fully upon him when he finished his work and stepped back into the receded shadow of the barn. And then he saw that he had hurt his hand. Though he did not know when he had hurt it, he knew how, for the memory now came vividly into his flesh. While he had been tightening the stud bolts that held the two machines together, using the large adjustable wrench that they called a knuckle-buster, the wrench, to which he had applied his whole weight and strength, slipped off the bolthead, and the middle knuckle of his right hand had struck the head of another bolt. Though he knew now, from the bloody tear in his flesh that the lick had been hard, what impressed him was that he had not been diverted by a hurt that not long ago he would have needed to show to the nearest older person for sympathy and perhaps a bandage.

And then a revelation came to him. All in a moment the anxious voices of his elders, their warnings, and certain reluctances belonging to himself, fell away from him, and he began to live by his own choice his own life, though he foresaw none of it, and though it would be another dozen years before he began actually the work that it would require of him.

The knowledge that came into him that morning

seemed to change him bodily. It came as exultation. He felt the tremor of it passing over him under his sweated clothes. He would remember that day when the time came for him to know and finally imagine the life of his grandpa Catlett, who had rejoiced in the good of it, even in the hardness of it, to his final day. And so Marce Catlett's ride home, beaten, broke, and elated, from the sale of his 1906 tobacco crop would come to light at last in his grandson's mind.

So Andy would take his own place within the so far ongoing force and determination of the story of the sale of his grandfather's work and pride for what his father called "a dirty low price."

# IX.

IN 1950, ANDY BECAME SIXTEEN YEARS OLD, eligible then for a driver's license, which he promptly acquired. And then for the next fourteen years—while he acquired further years of schooling, married, begat children, wandered away into the urban world that appeared to him then to be his destiny—he was distracted from the creaturely world of his grandfather Catlett that had formed and informed him, that his heart loved, and that was after all to be the dominant motive of his life.

As Marce Catlett's grandson and Wheeler Catlett's son, Andy was a born farmer, for whom good livestock and good pasture were lighted as the zenith, the very summer solstice, of human accomplishment. As his mother's son, Andy was a lover of reading and writing. Before he could read, she read to him and thereby gave permission and blessing to the book-reading he would do on his own. He learned to be pleased and to feel free when sitting somewhere by himself reading a book. He went back and forth in his enthusiasms between book-reading and the outdoor life and work of farming. He felt those as two kinds of freedom, which made him resentful of the confinement of school and therefore a poor student—a nuisance in fact to his schoolteachers because of his unscheduled questions and deliberate provocations.

His troublemaking and his poor grades finally caused his parents to send him away to a military school, which was less than a hundred miles away, in central Kentucky, but which at first seemed to him to be located utterly elsewhere, in a bad dream on the far side of the moon. He did not want to go, and his parents did not want to send him, but, as he pretty clearly knew, he had driven them to their wits' end, which is perhaps the school's exact location: Wits End Academy.

At that school he was at last noticed by two (two!) young teachers who saw something in him beyond the

## THE FORCE OF A STORY

knack for revolt. What they saw of course was his talent for reading and writing. They encouraged his reading of unassigned books. Under their influence he became the owner of a library of half a dozen cheap paperback books that he kept in a row on the shelf in his closet. His two sympathetic teachers, themselves readers of books, took note and were pleased.

Also they were puzzled by him. They thought him odd for his desire to be a farmer. They saw that as a boy headed inevitably into the modern world of cities and offices, he was handicapped by his country speech and ways. Because their affection for him was truly generous and honest, they tried to help him to know that the world's ways would not lead him back to where he had come from, for he could not amount to much of anything there. He saw a kind of reason in what they said. He thought they were undoubtedly right. And on some nights, thinking of his home country, his family, his friends by birthright, and of the coming time of his permanent absence, he would lie awake and grieve.

In those days nobody knew that he was a boy who belonged to a story. In those days he did not know it himself.

## MARCE CATLETT

He learned to work, in tobacco patches and hayfields, under the instruction and following the example of Elton Penn from the age of fourteen or so until at last, under his own instruction, he took charge of himself. He learned from Elton to work to finish work, not to "quitting time." "Weekend" was another concept foreign to Elton. Andy put himself to school to Elton Penn without understanding that a school was what it was.

Though it never declared itself as such, it was a school. It cohered, so long as it could and did, by Elton's deliberate mastery both of the new farm technology and the old curriculum that he then taught to, among others, Andy Catlett. Elton studied Marce Catlett for the short time he was able to know him, before Marce died in February of 1946, nearly two years after Elton became his neighbor. And until his own too early death in March of 1974, Elton studied Wheeler who also had studied Marce. So it was a school with scholarly lineage, coming from a kind of fascination, starting further back than anybody remembered: the never secure or final effort to hold on to the land. Wheeler studied Marce, his father; Elton studied Marce and Wheeler; Andy studied Marce and Wheeler as Elton helped him to know them, and he studied Elton.

---

# THE FORCE OF A STORY

Andy learned in high school at the same time the art of minimal compliance, intending to get away with whatever could be got away with. Insofar as his mind was capable at that time of having an intention that was not an instinct, he was intending to pass the courses that did not interest him with the least possible effort. To the courses that did interest him he gave what he thought was his best effort, though he had at the time no idea what his best effort might amount to. That, as it happened, he could not yet learn from himself.

From high school he went to the state university, not by any procedure of thought or judgment or even preference, but only because it was the most obvious place to go next, or as if it were the school most directly downhill from his high school. He went along much as before, though now less supervised and assuming pretty much that he was running his own show. As before, he worked with a sort of offhand care at the courses that interested him and applied the art of minimal compliance to those that did not, of which there were several.

He was going through his courses by "going through the motions," learning just enough about "subjects" and perhaps nothing about reality. But reality—to his surprise, of course—proved to be larger, even more generous, than he expected. Education is offered as courses; it is received as encounters with teachers and with subjects as known by teachers. Andy came to life mentally when he found at last two teachers standing square in his way: Albert Fairfield and Porter Ross, "Dr. Fairfield" and "Dr. Ross," as he would call them and learn to know them. They gave no sign that they were expecting him, but he discovered quickly that they had prepared for his arrival.

His teacher first and longest was Dr. Fairfield, who was passionate about the things he taught and who believed that students' mastery of subjects could best be demonstrated in essays. The essays did not have to extend to any set number of pages; they had only to be well made and complete. Dr. Fairfield surprised Andy by never accepting his work as good enough, and so requiring him to do it again and, frequently, yet again. Andy took several courses from Dr. Fairfield. A friendship grew between them that became affection that became eventually love, lifelong and perhaps longer. Andy had a way of asserting his independence that irritated and sometimes insulted his professors. Dr. Fairfield rebuked him: "Your arrogance is exceeded only by your ignorance!"—and consoled him, with a smile only somewhat ironic: "Whom the gods love, they chasten."

Dr. Ross came later, with a force of his own kind and contrivance. He wished it to be known, and he made sure it was known, that he was not a man to be fooled

# THE FORCE OF A STORY

with. At the end of one of Andy's last semesters, when final examinations were under way, Dr. Ross caught sight of Andy at work on another professor's exam. The allotted time had expired, and Andy was still writing—dawdling by Dr. Ross's standards. That watchman stepped two steps into the room and looked straight at Andy until Andy looked back. Dr. Ross hardened his stare. He said, "I'm going to *fix* you."

Andy knew he had been fairly warned. If he did not wish to be fixed by Dr. Ross, he had better fix himself.

There were three students in the class, such was the flavor of Dr. Ross's reputation. When the three were seated for the final, Dr. Ross handed Andy's two fellow students each a single page that appeared to Andy to be identically patterned by typescript. Without the slightest variation of momentum or expression, he handed three pages to Andy and stepped out of the room, not to return until the time was up.

And so Andy learned what Dr. Ross meant by "fix." His examination, made specifically for him, consisted of a hundred and twenty-five questions. The questions were not simple. They required thought. Even so, each of them could be—*had* to be—answered in a sentence or two. And Andy, who evidently had fixed himself well enough, answered them all and handed his paper to Dr. Ross at the end of the period.

Dr. Ross read Andy's exam as carefully as Andy had written it, refining his answers whenever possible, correcting several. At the top of the first page, he put an A-. Under the A- he wrote, "This has thought in it. I pay off for thought."

Porter Ross was a thorough teacher and an honest man, and so he, like Albert Fairfield, was thought to be "hard." But "hard" to a boy may be felt truly enough as hard. To Andy now, older by many years than they were when they were his teachers, "hard" has become the name of a right kind of duty and a right kind of love. The two of them required Andy to learn, though not yet what his best effort was, at least that he was capable of far better effort than he had so far thought. They forced him to learn the use of his mind. His memories of the two of them remain alive in his heart. He thanks them now maybe as they should be thanked, and with more than a return of love that has grown greater as he has grown older.

# X.

PERHAPS AS A SORT OF HOBBY, BUT FORTUNATELY, Andy took several courses in the College of Agriculture that, later, serving as "credentials," he happened to need. For the time eventually came when he submitted his ability to read and write along with his courses in "ag school" to a farming magazine published in Chicago. And so he achieved a good job and a living—the very future, as he realized, that the pair of his good teachers back in high school had anticipated for him.

His professors in the ag school, his colleagues on the staff of the magazine, and the magazine itself introduced him to a kind of farming that was far indeed from the farms that he had learned as ways of living from the people, dear to him, who had lived on them.

## MARCE CATLETT

His achievement, his very success, had moved him a world away from the influence of his grandfather and his father, of Elton Penn and the other friends and neighbors with whom he had worked during his boyhood and after. The new way of farming was not centered upon creatures but upon mechanical and chemical technologies. Its knowledge was scientific and commercial, not local, customary, and personal. When he traveled among the large industrializing farms of the Midwest in order to write about them, he saw little of the artistry and companionship that had so wakened his heart on the farms he had once known with a familiarity that seemed to him, looking back, to have been as much of his body as of his mind. In conversations among his colleagues and associates in the world of "agricultural journalism," several of whom introduced themselves as "old farm boys" or "old farm girls," he was surprised by how seldom they spoke of where they had come from.

And then he began to change. A change was coming into him that he at first resisted because he perceived it at first as backward. He resisted because the dominant assumption of his schooling had been in favor of

# THE FORCE OF A STORY

progress and the future. But his past self, which happened to be his true self, had begun to take form within him as for a second birth.

His employment, as he was coming to understand, was starkly factual and economic: an exchange, purely mathematical, of so much work for so much money, an arrangement, he began to see, that he could not love. He did not love his work. He did not love the heartless big farms he was paid to study and write about. In his agricultural travels, he had happened upon an exemplary Amish farm, eighty acres, beautifully kept, that had called to his heart. By a further good fortune, Flora, his wife, whose own calling was homeward, saw before he did that he had misplaced himself. He belonged, she told him, at home. If he was a writer, then he ought to go and live in the only subject of his own that he would ever have. His memory, wakened by her, came alive with the voices of his home-folks, among them his grandfather and his father, speaking with their great love for what he saw was a better kind of farming, still to an extent possible at home.

And so Andy and Flora, with their two children, gathered themselves and their possessions and moved—returned, as they felt—to the Catlett family's home neighborhood of Port William, which was, for that matter, the home neighborhood of the families of both of Andy's parents. They bought a small hillside farm, the old Riley Harford place on Harford Run, long neglected but familiar to Andy, fixed up its old stone house, and moved in.

If their homecoming was in a sense a step backward in time, it was economically a step downward. Andy no longer had a salary. In Mr. Milo Settle's terms, he had exchanged his "position" for a "job"—or, as it turned out, for a set of jobs, for all of the four members of his family. They had moved pretty much to the outer edge of what passed as American civilization, but not entirely beyond their need for money. To fill that need, Andy was able to transform his reading and writing into somewhat marketable articles, stories, lectures, and eventually books. Even so, to make a living at home, he and his family had to reduce wants in favor of needs, and they had to live to the extent possible from their land. For the comparative luxury of shopping at supermarkets they substituted a large garden, a flock of chickens, two milk cows, and two hogs for slaughter every fall. To minimize their use of heating oil, they purchased two wood-burning stoves that they fueled from their woodlands. As traction for farmwork, Andy forsook the recommended tractor for a team of horses, and thereby substituted their diet of mostly grass, which was cheap, for petroleum, which was expensive—and gained, into the bargain, an annual

# THE FORCE OF A STORY

tonnage of horse manure, for which their worn land was grateful. And so he renewed in his mind and mouth the language of his earliest teachers. Andy, who had seen and read enough of the fundamental, allegedly degrading work supplied by people thus degraded, took pride, and in fact a good deal of pleasure, in living directly from the work of his own hands. By doing so, he put into effect a democratic, anti-slavery, if not anti-racist, sentiment often spoken in the Port William neighborhood: "I won't ask another man to do for me anything I won't do for myself." But it was not Andy alone whose hands were at work. His hands now belonged to a family of hands, all reaching down into their home ground to raise their lives up out of it.

And so they took their place in the local life and economy of Andy's, and soon enough Flora's and their children's, home country. They came into the local life and economy that Andy's father had done much to preserve. They were at home with their neighbors in their neighborhood.

Andy began swapping work with people, now his neighbors, he had worked with starting in his boyhood: Elton and Mary Penn, Arthur and Martin Rowanberry,

Pascal and Sudie Rowanberry Sowers. They followed the only rule of membership: When any of them needed help, the others came to help. By extension of their one rule, there was no "settling up." All help was paid for in advance by the knowledge that there would be no end to anybody's need for help, which would be given to the limit of life and strength. To the economy of the homesteaders on the Harford place, this sharing of work was a vital support, always a comfort, often a joy. And it was profoundly instructive to Andy. Once he had begun farming a farm of his own, much that these older friends had said to him in the past revived and belonged in his mind and heart along with things they were saying to him now. They worked and they talked, their talk shaped by their work and by the country they were working in. And their talk seemed always open to laughter. Andy knew this also from his childhood: the grace and gracefulness of people talking for pleasure, their own and one another's.

What was his homecoming like for Andy? It was like being naked and cold and then getting into his clothes. One day when he was a boy, Andy was on one of his travels across the home place when he came by the pond in the back field. He had not had swimming on his mind, but there the pond was and there he was. In the sometimes strict economy of his pleasures, an

# THE FORCE OF A STORY

opportunity to swim was not to be wasted. And so he wasted no time in stripping off his clothes and diving in from the edge. He took his swim.

Before he went into the water, it had not mattered to him that the sky was overcast and a cool breeze was blowing. The breeze was not remarkably cool, but on his wet skin it felt cold. Of course he had nothing in the way of a towel. He had only the breeze to dry him, and by the time it had passably done do, he was shivering and clenching his teeth. When he put them on again, his clothes seemed to fit almost as perfectly as his skin, as if they remembered him and had retained his body's warmth.

It was like that, and like more than that, for when he came home he came again into the story and the stories of his family's life in that place, into which he also fitted, and which also gave a kind of warmth. In this absence his story, which was largely his family's story, had not quite become dormant in his mind. He had not quite departed from it. He had known that he was not just a man with a job. He knew he was a man whose story had been left at home. He had entered into the danger of recalling "typically country" fragments of his story to entertain his urban friends. Like a host of predecessors, he was selling his birthright for laughs or "shock value"—a danger escapable perhaps only by going home.

# XI.

ANDY COULD NOT HAVE UNDERSTOOD HIMSELF, his family, and his place as a puzzle put together for a longish time before he knew clearly what it was and how threatened it was. It was vulnerable and repeatedly threatened in families, as he knew because it had been so in his own family. But he realized also that the put-together puzzle was vulnerable in families now because of the vulnerability of its community. Until World War II, according to his memory and his memories of the memories of his elders, the Port William community was a put-together puzzle. Its people, most of them, understood themselves as its pieces. They spent much of their time, much of their lives, in telling its story. Their conversation, as they worked together and loafed in the loafing places of the town, was the living history of Port William, really its only record. Until World War II the town and countryside of Port William stayed at the center of its own attention. After the war it remained recognizably itself for a good many years, but its decline had become native to it. Year by year it became less than it had been. The elders died and were not replaced. Their children or grandchildren went away, returning only to bury their grandparents and then their parents.

Since his return, Andy has lived his story and his family's in that place for sixty years. The place as it was when he returned is no more. It is now, to him, a strange country with a familiar story surviving in it. Port William's fatal mistake was its failure to value itself at the rate of its affection for itself. Gradually, it had learned to value itself as outsiders—as the nation—valued it: as a "nowhere place," a place at the end of the wrong direction. So far as Andy has learned, the Old Order Amish, alone in all the country, have had the wisdom—the divine wisdom, it may be—to give to their own communities a value always primary and preserved by themselves.

Andy could not have understood his father until he had understood his grandfather. He could not have

## THE FORCE OF A STORY

understood his grandfather until he had understood his father. He could not have understood his father until he had understood the tobacco program and himself as one among its beneficiaries. And he supposes that he could not have completed his understanding of his grandfather and his father until he understood, more or less, himself as he is now, having, like them and with them, grown old—the three of them united by their efforts, so far failed, to establish a sufficient, reasonably self-sufficient, permanent, inheritable, and renewable farm life in a beloved place. This has been for each of them a powerful vision and desire: modest, entirely reasonable, but still a possibility out of reach.

Before his grandfather's generation, Andy thinks, an authentically settled life in place was not possible because of chattel slavery and its malign influence on everything within its horizon. Slavery was, and it is, correctable only by the courage to connect freedom with responsibility. By "responsibility" Andy has understood the ability and the readiness to do one's own work and to clean up one's own messes. That—only that—is anti-slavery. Maybe it can come at last when we have finished with "mobility"—which, despite its several reasons, has always permitted the mobile ones to shed their mistakes in one place by moving off to a "new start" in another place.

The point is that if the puzzle of a community in place is put together and kept together long enough, it will work out on its own the terms and conditions of its coherence through time and change. It will need no outside help, no expert advice. Of this the human past furnishes plenty of examples, all of them no doubt imperfect, but instructive even in their imperfections.

It is similarly true that if rural people were to be paid justly for their work and their products, and if most of them should remain together in place, they themselves would solve the so-called rural problems. An example of this is Andy Catlett's own home country during the best decades of the burley tobacco economy.

In stable and lasting communities, people become neighbors to one another because they need one another. The American story so far—which has been so far the Catletts' story, which they have both suffered and resisted—has been the fairly continuous overpowering of the instinctive desire for settling and homemaking by the forces of unsettling: the westward movement, land greed, money hunger, false economy. The industrial replacement of neighborhood by competition and technology moves everything worthy of love out of reach.

It is nonetheless true that within a settled community any good accomplished by an individual or a group or a generation might be taken up and preserved as a

# THE FORCE OF A STORY

part of its culture and economy. When a community is unsettled, nothing good can last very long.

The Burley Tobacco Growers Co-operative Association, which had existed somewhat tentatively since 1920, was reorganized under the New Deal in 1940. Andy's father was actively involved in its revival and in its life afterward. The New Deal was not perfect of course, but it did in part fulfill a government's responsibility to provide needed protections that the people cannot provide for themselves. The tobacco program was a part of a public-supported governmental effort to conserve soil and preserve farmers. Though it was a governmental program, it was given into the responsibility of local leaders. That was the genius of it, as far at least as Andy's home country was concerned. Unlike the coal economy of eastern Kentucky, which was imposed upon the land and people by economic adventurers from elsewhere, the burley tobacco economy was regional and local. Its leaders were homegrown, and they stood up for the common life and the common good. And so that economy grew up from the land by the fairly paid, therefore caring, work of the land's people. Because of that, its effect upon that region was conserving and democratic.

It was, in spirit and performance, an agrarian program. By way of it, Wheeler Catlett and his colleagues took the longest, firmest step so far toward the stability that their people had needed and, in a time now gone, had desired.

Then came the great fulcrum of World War II. Coming up to it was the public will and wish to correct historical mistakes in the treatment of farmland and farmers. The war and the war effort maintained the favorable reputation of farmers: Under the circumstances, their contribution to the common good was obvious. But the great and permanent domestic results called forth by the war were advances in technology and manufacturing. The machines and chemicals, required in prodigal quantities as weapons of war, could as well be fitted to the requirements, "scientifically" oversimplified, of agriculture. And so began the all-out industrialization of rural America. The new ways of farming were in fact new kinds of mining: maximum production at minimal expense, extraction without maintenance or any return of care. It was a foreign invasion, the homecoming of the war, except that the invaders now were the industrial corporations of urban America, employing rural labor as cheaply as possible to establish what has remained a domestic colonialism.

# THE FORCE OF A STORY

The use and care even of the small-featured landscapes, the slopes and swales, swells and creases of Andy's home country, began to change at the war's end. The good, frugal famers who drove their first tractors into the fields around Port William were entering, without knowing it, the technological romance of the corporate giants, the millionaires and the billionaires, who would conquer the earth, conquer "space," invade Mars, a place better known to them than the country that grows their food. (This is now a policy of the second Trump administration.) Andy did not learn of this from hearsay or reading. He saw it and lived in it from the start. For years, even decades, the farmers who were Andy's teachers and exemplars, though they made the change to tractors, kept to their old ways, maintaining their household economies, caring well for their land and living from it, keeping up the helps and pleasures of their neighborhoods. But Andy saw too that more and more people, once hardened to farm life and the weather, cheerfully accepting of the work, skilled at it, proud of it, began a reluctance toward it that was new. They began—the older people slowly, the young at once—to work with their minds diverted to quitting time or Saturday night, places where the lights were bright and the good times rolled. So it went. One by one, the old-fashioned, proud, self-helping, neighbor-helping, truly agrarian farmers, who had been Andy's workmates, his teachers, and his great companions, came separately to the outside door, departed, and were not replaced.

# XII.

IT HAS BEEN A LONG TIME, NEARLY TWENTY years, since the federal program for burley tobacco was formally ended. And it has been a longer time since the best years of that program. As perspective lengthens, it becomes possible to look back over the program's history in the Catlett family's home country, and to see it whole. For Andy Catlett this has become a need, partly because so much of his own history is at one with the crop and the history of the program, and partly because in the course of the program's best years he took it and its results too much for granted.

Growing up on the margins of his elders' lives, overhearing their talk, especially his father's talk, he learned more than he knew he was learning, about tobacco and other things. And then he became a big boy, big enough at least to be set to work in the crop, and he learned more. But it took him years, even as a grownup, to understand fully that the widely shared modest prosperity of the farms and small towns of the country he grew up in, while he was growing up, was not simply the way of the world. It was an economy deliberately made and fitted to the nature and needs of its region by the Burley Tobacco Growers Co-operative Association. It is important to understand how well-suited the program was in the early 1940s to the farms, the farmers, their staple crop, and their culture as they were at that time.

Burley tobacco was the staple crop of its region even before the tobacco program made it reliably so, because the people who grew it loved it and loved the art of making it "fine," the adjective by which it was customarily praised. The land of its region gave it uniquely the color and flavor that made it desirable to manufacturers. And so the art of producing it was a collaboration between the farmer, his family and neighbors, and the soil of their "tobacco patches."

A good crop of burley tobacco in those days was a work of art. The artistry of it consisted of many steps through the growing season, and before and after each one, depending on knowledge, judgment, and generations of experience. It took thirteen months, they used

# THE FORCE OF A STORY

to say, to raise a crop of tobacco. That saying gave a certain pleasure, but it was not entirely a joke, for the end of the work of one crop year did in Andy's earliest years often overlap with the work that began the next.

In late winter or earliest spring—during, let us say, the 1940s—the farmers gathered fuel from the woods and elsewhere with which to burn the plant beds. The plant beds were a hundred feet long by nine or twelve feet wide. They would be broken, harrowed, and smoothed to make the finest sort of seedbed, and then they would be burned. The gathered wood was laid on the beds and set afire, and the fire would be spread evenly over the worked surface to sterilize the ground and destroy seeds. A sort of beautiful geography was laid upon the country at night during that time. From the heights of the land, you could see the fires of the burning plant beds far and wide. You would know that people were sleepless and busy around every one of them, moving the coals and the firebrands about to make the burning as even as possible.

After the fire would come the seed. At the right time, still early in the year, the tiny seeds would be sown into the beds, which then would be covered with "canvas," a thin cotton mesh pinned to the ground by bent wires pushed through metal grommets along the edges. The canvas would protect the plants against the frosty or freezing nights that were still to come, and then against the hot sunshine.

When the seedling plants were up and fully visible, the beds had to be painstakingly weeded. People would sit or lie, often on sacks of straw, along the beds' edges. This work was so closely attentive and detailed as to resemble sewing or reading. Sometimes you needed the point of a blade of your pocket knife to remove the weed seedlings from among the tobacco seedlings. This was the quietest kind of work, frequently done by several people working together, and so of course there would be talk—the beginning, you might say, of that year's conversation. In the Port William neighborhood until World War II ended in 1945, and for while after, there were almost no tractors. The whole crop was achieved in a quiet now hard to imagine but good for conversation.

To understand tobacco, the year-round demanding presence of it, the culture of it, you have to know that it was, above all others, a convivial crop. Several times a year it called for crew work, the crews usually made up of family members and neighbors, and always there would be talk. There were a lot of good talkers in those days. The crop could not be accomplished without hard

# THE FORCE OF A STORY

work, but it offered pleasures too, and conversation was one of them.

When the beds needed weeding, they would be weeded, or "wed," as some would say. If the weather was dry, the young plants would need water, and water would be hauled to them in barrels to be splashed lightly onto the canvas from a dipped pan or the end of a siphon.

Once the ground and the weather were warm, usually in late May, the plants, their white stems grown maybe to the thickness of a pencil, would be drawn from the beds to be "set" regularly in the fields, or "patches," as they were called. In preparation, the patches would have been "laid off" in rows deeply inscribed in the worked and leveled soil. If the weather remained dry, the plants would be set with the help of a mechanical transplanter, a "tobacco setter," drawn by a steady team of horses or mules. If it rained, making a "tobacco season," the crew worked barefooted, setting the plants into the marked rows by hand. A boy or a girl, typically, would go in front, dropping the plants from a basket carried on a forearm, and one of the men, best if he was young, would come along behind, setting the plants into holes opened with a wooden peg, a "tobacco peg," or the setter's thumb, and closing the earth upon the roots. The work stayed answerable to a need to hurry—to get the crop into the ground and growing, the sooner the better, but often also because the setters, at least the younger ones, might be inclined to race. The setters bent to their work at the start of a row and did not straighten their backs until the end. And so they needed the plants to be dropped at the correct intervals along the rows, and their patience tended to be short. A dropper who dropped the plants too close together or too far apart was apt to be somewhat sharply instructed. A boy who worked too slow might feel the peg striking close to his bare heels.

From the time the plants were in the ground until their leaves had nearly met between the rows, the patches would be cultivated by plow and hoe, the plow working between the rows and the hoe between and closely around the plants. The intention simply was that the patch should be weedless. It was no surprise to hear a scrupulous tobacco man say, "I clean my crop for the same reason I wash my face," and with an emphasis that put the issue beyond question.

The most damaging pests were hornworms and

budworms. At the time of this account, these were often removed by hand. But in the 1940s insecticides were coming into use, beginning with Paris green.

As the plants began to mature, but usually before they bloomed, they would be "topped" by breaking or cutting off the top of the stalk along with a few of the upper leaves. This brought to further growth and maturity the leaves of commercial size and quality. It also caused the plant to grow "suckers" at the axils of all the remaining leaves. At the right time these would be broken out, leaving only the top two. Leaving those two prevented the regrowth of suckers lower down. The top two would remain and grow until immediately before harvest, allowing the plant itself to mature and "ripen."

At harvest the plants were cut by hand, one at a time, and placed on "tobacco sticks." These were slender wooden staves, split or sawed, best if split, four feet long, and supposed to be (but not always) sharpened on at least one end so as to be stuck easily upright in the ground. In the early 1940s the stalks still were split and straddled onto the sticks. By 1950, the splitting knife had been replaced by a light hatchet, a "tomahawk," and the cut stalks were pierced and slid onto the stick by means of a hollow metal spear, which the cutter fitted onto the end of each stick as he (sometimes she) came to it. A stick at that time held six plants. Cutters were expected, or they expected themselves, to handle the plants tenderly so as not to break or bruise the leaves.

The tobacco cutting was the crisis of the crop year. It required the hardest work, and the greatest care. After they were cut and before they were "housed" in the curing barn, the plants were vulnerable both to the heat of the sun and to rain. They could be sunburned, which would discolor the leaves and so impair their worth. And rain, depending of course on its amount and intensity, could do several kinds of damage. It was best for several reasons, weather permitting, to allow the cut plants to wilt somewhat before they were taken to the barn. Wilted, the sticks of tobacco handled and loaded better, and there was less chance of deterioration after they were housed.

People who worked in the tobacco harvest day after day and year after year were not surprised by the need, now and then, to haul and house wet tobacco, which meant working in wet clothes. That would add one more discomfort to work that was already uncomfortable. But the remarkable thing about this work, hard as it might be, was that you got used to it. And just at the hardest, hottest, most miserable, most troublesome

# THE FORCE OF A STORY

moment of a long afternoon, somebody would render a complaint of exceeding eloquence or make a joke or recall something funny that somebody had said at such a moment in another year, and then everybody would be gathered into a passage of laughter that would lead to more talk and more laughter, until the whole miserable bunch, without noticing how it had happened, would be enjoying themselves.

One day, after the passing of the tobacco economy, Andy Catlett met his neighbor Tommy Sowers in town. He said, "Tommy, what was the last year we cut tobacco together?"

"I don't know," Tommy said. "I can't tell you right off. But you know, I miss them old times."

The men who loaded the wagons that carried the sticks of tobacco from patch to barn, needed to know what they were doing. Always, unendingly, the pressure was on to handle the tobacco carefully. Not a leaf should be broken or torn or bruised—let alone stepped on. (If you were a boy who stepped on a leaf, you would be not very politely encouraged to be mindful of your feet.) No detail was beneath notice. The load had to be built so that it would keep its shape and stay loaded during the sometimes jolty trip to the barn. But the loader also would want to make a load that looked well. Though the phrase "pretty work" came often enough into the talk, nobody spoke much of beauty. But this work of the tobacco harvest, when rightly done, was beautiful at every step and stage. Nobody wanted to be guilty of making something unsightly of any part of it. To the minds best attuned to the crop and the work, any mess was a "damned mess." Beauty was the goal—beauty and the satisfaction it gave.

In the barn, unloading the wagons and hanging the sticks of tobacco in the tiers, the artistry was sustained, even intensified. Farmers of the 1940s, though the tiers by then were mostly two-by-fours, still spoke of "tier poles," for the barns, earlier, had been tiered with straight poles cut from the woods. In the 1940s and later, you might work at times in old barns still tiered with such poles or even with old fence rails, and then you had to be careful. The tiers were spaced about three and three-quarters feet apart horizontally, and vertically. Under the highest pitch of the roof, there might be six tiers at vertical intervals of three or four feet. To house the tobacco, men (or big boys) would stand on the tiers, straddling the spaces between them, in a vertical row of two or three. The sticks would be handed from the wagon to the man in the bottom tiers, who would

# THE FORCE OF A STORY

hang some in "his" tiers and hand others, in order, to the hand or two working above, so that the tiers filled evenly from one end to the other, and every stalk hung freely.

The focus of attention now was air circulation. The sticks were regularly spaced along the tiers, the stalks regularly spaced on the sticks. Nothing, not a loose or a turned-up leaf, was to block the free flow of air around each plant. The owner of the crop would most likely be at work with the others, and most likely more than the others he would be worrying about the variety of rot called "house burn" that in hot, muggy weather might start with a badly handled plant and spread to others. He would be keeping an eye on everything, correcting, cautioning, and encouraging. He might call up to the boy housing the top tier, "Pull the end of that stick a little toward you, Tom Cat." Or, "Andy, look what you're doing, now." Or he might sing out, "Take 'em and shake 'em and regu-late 'em."

No painter could have had a more schooled and unresting eye for detail than the farmer who had earned the rank of "tobacco man," a title not easily earned and always spoken with respect. Once his crop had been brought safely in, out of the weather, a great worry was lifted from him, and his thoughts could venture ahead into the farm's other season-ending work. He might wonder now about the condition of his overshoes or his winter underwear. But until the tobacco was cured or nearly so, he kept alert to the weather, opening or shutting the doors and ventilators of the barn according to his estimate of the need. Coke stoves were sometimes fired beneath the hanging tobacco to speed the flow of air and to remove excess moisture from plants newly housed.

When the crop was cured and at rest, so to speak, there was not yet any rest for the farmer. In the highly diverse farming of those years, the field work continued well into the fall. The tobacco ground, now bare, had to be harrowed and seeded with wheat or barley and bluegrass. The corn had to be cut and shocked, and eventually shucked and cribbed. The corn ground had to be harrowed and seeded. And then there might come a breathing spell. Back in those days, Andy Catlett's friends Arthur and Martin Rowanberry, their father and brothers, always put in two weeks of hunting between the end of the corn harvest and the start of tobacco stripping. Those two weeks gave them a freedom, a long breath of the open air, that they needed before their long confinement in the stripping room.

# THE FORCE OF A STORY

For the tobacco crop, the year was yet far from ended. The time would come when it required a "season," a day or so when damp weather would bring the tobacco "into case," allowing the dried and brittle leaves to absorb moisture from the air and become pliable. Then the hanging tobacco could be dropped without damage from the tiers to the barn floor. The stalks then would be removed from the sticks, tightly "bulked" ("booked") and covered so as to keep the leaves moist and pliant enough to handle.

In those days before rural electrification, a stripping room had a long row of north-facing windows that lighted a broad bench, continuous from one end of the room to the other. The stalks of tobacco would be carried in armloads from the bulk into the room and piled high onto the left-hand end of the bench. One by one, the stalks were taken from the pile and passed along the bench as the leaves were removed. The bench was divided, though not by visible marks, into four sections, at each of which somebody stood at work. The leaves were taken from the stalks in four different grades, according to consistency and color, which explains the need for light from the north windows. Starting with the leaves at the butt or lower end of the stalk, which were removed at the left-hand end of the bench, the grades were: spodge, lug, red, and tip. Each of the four workers stripped one of the grades. The lugs, the grade that was most valuable, were the longest leaves, a bright tan in color, thought to be, as they were, the most beautiful. The stalk was held in the left hand as the right hand did the stripping. The stem ends of the leaves accumulated in the right hand as it pulled them off. When the right hand had gathered as many leaves as it comfortably could hold, the worker would select a "tie leaf" and use it to bind the stem ends tightly together, producing what was known as "a hand of tobacco." The finished crops of that era are said to have been "tied in hands."

When tied, the hand was straddled onto a tobacco stick that was kept protruding from the edge of the bench. When the stick was well filled, it was placed in a "tobacco press," which flattened the hands under heavy pressure, causing them to adhere tightly and flatly together. From the press, the "stripped sticks" were laid neatly into another bulk, from which they would be carried to market. When the last stick had gone into that bulk, only then, at long last, could the farmer consider that he had "raised a crop of tobacco."

The stripping rooms were equipped with stoves, and so they were comfortable in cold weather. That made it

# THE FORCE OF A STORY

possible—and it was a common thing in those days—for a family to move its daytime life into the stripping room when all hands were needed there. While the mother worked at the bench, her baby or babies might occupy a crib or playpen close at hand. Children a little older would be playing in the stripping room and the barn and outside and around.

   Standing at the bench hour after hour, day after day, it might be for two or three months, was hard work, which required constant judgment and discrimination and yet was monotonous. And so just as constantly there would be talk. Stories would be told, returned to for correction or elaboration, and perhaps told again. A stripping room was a good place to visit, for visitors were welcome, as was anything that brought laughter. The talk that went with the conviviality of the tobacco crop never stopped until the tobacco economy and the crop itself departed from the small farms. And then everything changed, for there is no denying the dependence of local culture upon local economy and local work.

It would be of considerable historical interest, insofar as it would be possible, to understand the influence of burley tobacco on the life of Andy Catlett and others of his generation who came of working age in the tobacco patches of the late 1940s and early 1950s, and its influence as well on their communities. This is of interest because in the 1950s and decades before and after, that crop provided to the mostly small farmers who raised it, and to their communities, not only an economic basis but also the form and substance of a local and regional way of life like no other.

No other crop demanded such continuous attention over so long a time. No other required so much and such elaborate knowledge, or such refinement of perception and judgment, or such artistry of management and handling. It seems doubtful that in the modern world any other product depended for its production upon such a level of artistry that was generally or democratically distributed. The crop was grown mainly in small acreages on small farms. A farm of two hundred acres would have been considered fairly large, and a farm of that size might have had, under the program, a tobacco allotment, or "base," of three or four acres. And so the crop, its interest, and its work shaped the minds, seasons, and lives of every farmer of its region.

As a crop grown in small acreages, on the right scale, it was a family crop. Children followed their parents in the work and so learned to know the work, the crop, their parents, and themselves. At critical times when crew work was needed, the neighbors came in to help, thus neighbors learned one another, and from one another. And so the crop developed necessarily and naturally its own language.

By its language, by the elaborate knowledge that the work of it required, by its history as it lived on in living memory, by its year-round presence in time and consciousness, the crop gave a culture to the people of its region. Though the tobacco crop and tobacco culture were in obvious ways different, they were inseparable. When the crop, as a family and neighborly enterprise on small farms, disappeared from the country, its culture also disappeared. There was of course some public talk of "finding a replacement for tobacco," but nothing could replace it.

When you have a crop, and a culture, that gives employment at home to whole families, that puts the children to work with their parents, that helps you to raise your children, and you lose it all at once and have nothing to replace it, then what?

Andy Catlett received a letter from a young man who knew from experience what he was talking about: "They're asking what comes next after tobacco and the tobacco program. I can tell them what's next. Dope." Yes, it was dope. And other ailments. Tobacco has been gone now for twenty years. Nothing has replaced it. Its absence is a damage that people here will be trying to survive, repair, and get over longer than they can foresee.

# XIII.

THE REGION IN WHICH BURLEY TOBACCO WAS grown varied in topography from gently "rolling" in central Kentucky to varyingly hilly. The crop was exceedingly "labor-intensive." In 1949, when wheat required 5 hours of work per acre, corn 19 hours, and cotton 83 hours, an acre of tobacco required 460 hours,* or 46 10-hour days, and this partly was because of the unrelenting emphasis at that time (and long after) upon quality. For those reasons, partly, the crop was grown mainly in small acreages on small farms.

Another reason, also crucial, was that the program's

---

\* I "came upon" those numbers. I don't know how reliable they are.

bias favored a fairly democratic distribution of the allotments and kept the allotments attached to the farms rather than to the farmers. That ended in 1971. The demands of the growers had shifted, with the enlargement of their technology, toward larger acreages. The old agrarian standards had been replaced by measures of power, speed, and size. The allotment per farm, measured at first in acres and then in pounds, was set by the program in accordance with the previous history of production on that farm. After 1971, allotments could be accumulated into larger acreages.

In the 1940s and for several decades following, the farms of the burley region were highly diversified, producing often on the same farm cattle, sheep, and hogs, in addition, during the 1940s, to the work animals. Enough corn was grown, typically, to feed the resident livestock. The corn and tobacco would be followed by bluegrass and clover or alfalfa. Farm families of that time typically lived as much as possible from the produce of their farms. And of course they helped themselves to nature's free provender from the fields and the woods, ponds, and streams. They lived frugally, spending little, saving more than spending.

To such an economy, the tobacco income, kept at parity and made dependable by the program, provided a basis that was solid and sound. The regional economy at that time was not rich, but it was steadily and widely prosperous, securing the farm population on the farms,

# THE FORCE OF A STORY

making it possible for tenant farmers to buy farms, and providing employment in the towns as on the farms for everybody who wanted to work.

Burley tobacco, the regional economy, and the way of farming that it belonged to, that in a way belonged to it, provided the most continuous and coherent course in Andy Catlett's fundamental education, which lasted until he was grown and in his thoughts has never come to rest. From the time he was able to walk around under his own guidance, he played in the presence of the crop as the work of it was being done, played at doing the work and so learned to do the work, and by the age of fourteen became finally worthy to be hired to do the grownup work of it for pay. That was when his friend and neighbor Elton Penn started him cultivating the newly rooted and growing crop with a walking plow behind a learned old mule known as Tank. He seems still to be learning from it now in his old age as it all returns to mind, the work in its complexity and comeliness, the teachers and companions with whom he worked and talked and laughed. To his surprise, sometimes will come to him again the memory of how it was in some moment of some old day he thought he had forgotten, the angle of the light, the motion of the air, a voice calling, a voice answering, the loveliness of it.

## MARCE CATLETT

He sees also, looking back, that the crop and the way of living it supported were doomed. The reasons are obvious. The crop became indefensible because of its identification as a cause of cancer. Following that, the quality of the product and its production ceased to count economically, and therefore culturally, as it had before. For bad reasons, acreages were getting larger, and migrant labor was coming in. The farmers' children were leaving the farms. Once the program was ended at last by the so-called conservatism that had always opposed it, the crop was already ceasing to support the regional pattern of diversified small farms. And then the countryside had no protection against invasion by large acreages of soybeans and corn, a ruin long established in the Midwest, and even more alien and ruinous in Andy Catlett's homeland. The small dairy farms were being put out of business by the growth of larger dairies elsewhere. Herds of beef cattle on family-size farms are keeping still a significant portion of the land in pasture, and so preserving an old kind of love and a kind of hope, but so far that way of farming is dependent on town jobs. The countryside, once all astir with the life of closely neighboring farmsteads and fields, has become a place where few people work, where city workers sleep.

—

# THE FORCE OF A STORY

As an effect of several causes, including professional and official advice, the traditional subsistence economies of households and neighborhoods were supplanted by the global economy of extraction, consumption, and waste. Homemade goods, derived from the homeland and handwork, were replaced by purchased goods dependent upon "purchasing power."

By those errors the country people were gathered into cities, or into the city economy even when they remained in the country. Thus they were exiled from their homelands, their histories and memories, their self-subsistent local economies, thus becoming more ignorant and dependent than people ever have been before. And so they made perhaps the worst error of all: a bothways exile of the living from the dead.

As people have grown helpless and lonely, they have come to be governed by the most wealthy, who rule by the purchase of nominal representatives, who, having no longer the use of their own minds, do not know and cannot imagine the actual country by the ruin of which they and their constituents actually live.

## XIV.

NO PART OF THE HISTORY OF THE COUNTRY during Andy's lifetime is remote from him, for he has lived it, almost all of it, as a countryman in the country where that history has taken place. It is a history not dividable from the story of his life. It is not dividable from his family's story as it has proceeded from that day many winters ago when Marce Catlett's hogsheads of tobacco, his many days of hope and work, put nothing in his pocket. The history of their time is Andy's family's story because Marce's story, becoming Wheeler's story and that of the generations following, has held them in place. It has turned them back out of one absence after another, one generation after another, so far, to work still unfinished at home. That man, standing then for himself, stands for a myriad of others who have stood in the same enforced passivity to accept too little as the price of their work, saying not a word.

Andy has come at last to see his grandfather Catlett, his father, and himself as three aged brothers made so by their shared vision of a life permanently settled in a place chosen and beloved, but made brothers also by their failure: their discovery that the vision, as each one of them in his own time has seen it, could not live beyond them, so hard upon them has been the force of the changing of times. Past each of them, as his strength failed and the way of nature opened before him, the vision would have to be taken up again, seen again in a changed light, renewed by a younger effort. The three of them as old men are bound together by a common ground, a common vision, and a common failure. But Andy was both greatly moved and somewhat bewildered by his seeing them as brothers, implying a simultaneousness or a continuousness of thought, as among contemporaries. What had he meant?

And then he remembered his other grandfather, Mat Feltner, saying to him, seeming to remember, "There was a time when Chicago burned to the ground, and in

# THE FORCE OF A STORY

Port William we didn't hear of it for weeks." Andy forgot that, and then he remembered it again when he happened upon the year of the Chicago fire: 1871, a dozen years before his grandfather Feltner was born. And so Mat Feltner had been speaking as Ben Feltner, his father, while he was speaking for himself. And so Andy has had to see himself, grown old, a man of his own time who might say as if born a century before his birth, "There was a time when Chicago burned, and in Port William we didn't hear of it for weeks." Or who could say, "What we wanted was to make a life and a way of life, here in this place, that our children and their children could take from us and carry on. And each of us, in his own way in his own time, has failed."

As Andy's years accumulated and his strength could no longer answer the demands of the hillside farm that had been home and life to his marriage and a school to his children and grandchildren, he began to waken into his memory and the memories of his elders. It was as if his soul had learned, so to speak, to stand outside his own life in the great opening in which time comes and goes, in the company and council of fellow souls. In reveries and dreams he makes his way among loved ones lost to one another in this world's great sundering, as if again in their presence and present to them, as if in some hereafter already here.

His remembering and his thoughts have carried him by now far outside the matter of fact of this world's present age. He stands now with his father and his father's father, and with others dear to them, in the presence of a longed-for beautiful land that they have desired as if seen afar, that yet is the same, the very land that they have known and that they know, a love-made land, dark to them until by their own love they came to see it.

Andy's life, like the history of his home country in his time, has divided into two parts, the first agrarian and creaturely, the second industrial and mechanical. But the two parts do not fit together so as to make one whole. They are the two parts of one life and one history, but they are as if insistently or resistantly different from each other—or, as Andy supposes them to be, opposed to each other. The parts are joined, it seems to him, only by the strand of his own diminishing life, compounded of the lives of his grandfather Catlett and his father and of others, many others, and only by the diminishing life

## THE FORCE OF A STORY

of the country, continuing by the spirit and the breath of God toward whatever in God's time it is coming to.

And so he prays his benediction and farewell to Marce Catlett's establishment of his effort upon their home place that Wheeler and then Andy were born to, the placed and singular effort lost to them in the stampede of machinery and chemistry that followed the so far greatest war—his requiem, maybe it is, not for the hard-worn old house as it used to be, the cellar, the smokehouse, the hen house, the garden divided by a grape arbor down the middle, not the barn with its stalls and mule pen, the cow stall, the corn crib, the granary, the hog pen, the wagon shed, the wells deep dug and walled, not those, but the way that once lived among them, the paths worn and wearing day by day, that connected them during a lifetime to one man's effort and desire.

# XV.

OF THE ARTIFACTS OF THE OLD LIFE, IT IS THE cellar just outside and handy to the kitchen door, sunk into the ground and rising from it, that Andy most mourns, because it is the most lost and most needing to be remembered: the hollow of it dug down below frost, the dome of it laid up of fragments of the layered limestone that the country was founded on. The builder was most likely an Irish or Scottish stonemason, by the mystery of whose art the heavy rocks could be held by their own weight aloft, to be the roof of a somewhat sunken room maybe a dozen feet in diameter, maybe eight feet from the center of the floor to the vent that opened at the crest of the dome. Andy's mourning here becomes the wish to step again down into the semi-darkness of that room with a carpenter's ruler to order his memory by the exact dimensions. It was anyhow an ample dome, built of courses of rocks rising and curving inward toward a keystone at the top. The dome of rocks, laid with their straightest edges aligned evenly on the inside, was covered deeply on the outside with the earth of the excavation, and smoothly plastered on the inside. The vent at the top opened to the air by way of a brick chimney, of which the highest bricks were laid in an arch to keep out the rain. The earthen exterior was shored up by a rock wall that went all the way around.

The cellar was entered by way of a brick anteroom with, by Andy's time, a green-painted tin roof. You stepped through the door and then, between broad stone shelves, down stone steps onto the concrete floor. The room was cool and dry in the summer, in the winter dry and warm, dimly but sufficiently lighted by the opened door. Its most remarkable feature was a shelf, waist-high and a foot and a half wide, that extended around the whole circumference. It was composed of large flagstones keyed into the wall, their straight sides aligned, and like the wall smoothly plastered. This provided Grandma Catlett a place to store her canned goods, and in the warm months to set her crocks of fresh milk, morning and evening, to wait for the cream to rise.

# THE FORCE OF A STORY

The cellar imprinted itself on Andy's memory when he was a boy. He played on the grassy hump of it, sat on the retaining wall in the shade of an elm tree that had grown up beside it, followed his elders down into it. He was in a way charmed by it. He *liked* it. He has given much time to understanding and appreciating it in its absence.

Its principal structure, the dome, overlaid with earth and a further cover of grass, was virtually imperishable. And this was the result of an elegant reconciliation of art and nature. Its existence and its durability were the results of an enforced beauty. If the dome of rocks had not been beautifully made, it could not have been made: it could not have held together to the end of its making. The beauty of it was not as evident as that of a vault or dome in a church, but it was beautiful, both materially and in thought. It was in every sense a work of art, and as such it was unique. The same builder could not have built it quite the same again as it was. It could not be even approximately reproduced now when the ancient art of it has been lost.

Now it has disappeared and the ground is level where it was. It might have endured and remained useful for many years, even centuries. But it was old, it was thing of the past, and in the age of the bulldozer it was in the way.

## MARCE CATLETT

As he has come to know, Andy's grief for the things that are lost affirms his love for them, as even the loss of them affirms the bounty by which they once existed, for in this world grief goes hand in hand with gratitude.

And yet this world, in which time and change are the way of life, has suffered and so far survived five centuries of global conquest and plunder. Greed has passed to and fro over the whole earth, reducing life to matter and matter to price. Though time and change bring sorrow, they belong to the seasons, to fecundity and health, but greed is a mortal disease.

The history of the Port William countryside, like that of the world since 1492, has included so much disgrace and destruction that the continuation so far of the life of it, and of the beauty still of so much of it, seems to Andy to be a wonder almost equal to the wonder of its creation in the beginning. It is a wonder to him that he and his people have been spared so far the just consequence of their folly. He thinks that a great patience and a great forgiveness must so far have been in force, and he gives thanks.

## THE FORCE OF A STORY

He gives thanks for life continuing on the earth, and for the earth continuing alive. He gives thanks for the continuing so far of his own life, the story of which, as he knows it, is longer than his life, for it began a generation before his birth and may continue past his death in generations for whom, if they remain in place, the story will be a landmark as they remember it and continue it.

As they have carried the story, the dead and the living have been carried by it through the breakages of broken times, circling generation by generation back to that distant land, which they have never reached except by trial and in spells, never yet placing two generations securely in succession, the land where more than a century ago Marce Catlett departed with cautious hope in the dark past midnight, came home broke, and in the dark before daylight the next morning went back to work.

# ACKNOWLEDGMENTS

This book is based upon a "real story," which, because it is mostly undocumented, must be told as fiction. In writing it, I have relied on family stories, my own memories, and my long conversations with Tom Grissom. Tom, I think, will remain the most thorough student of the history of the Burley Tobacco Growers Co-operative Association. I am indebted to him for both the knowledge and the pleasure I took from our conversations.

WENDELL BERRY, an essayist, novelist, and poet, has been honored with the T. S. Eliot Prize, the Aiken Taylor Award in Modern American Poetry, the John Hay Award of the Orion Society, and the Dayton Literary Peace Prize, Richard C. Holbrooke Distinguished Achievement Award, among other distinctions. In 2010, he was awarded the National Humanities Medal by President Barack Obama, and in 2016, he was the recipient of the Ivan Sandrof Life Achievement Award from the National Book Critics Circle. Berry lives with his wife, Tanya Berry, on their farm in Henry County, Kentucky.

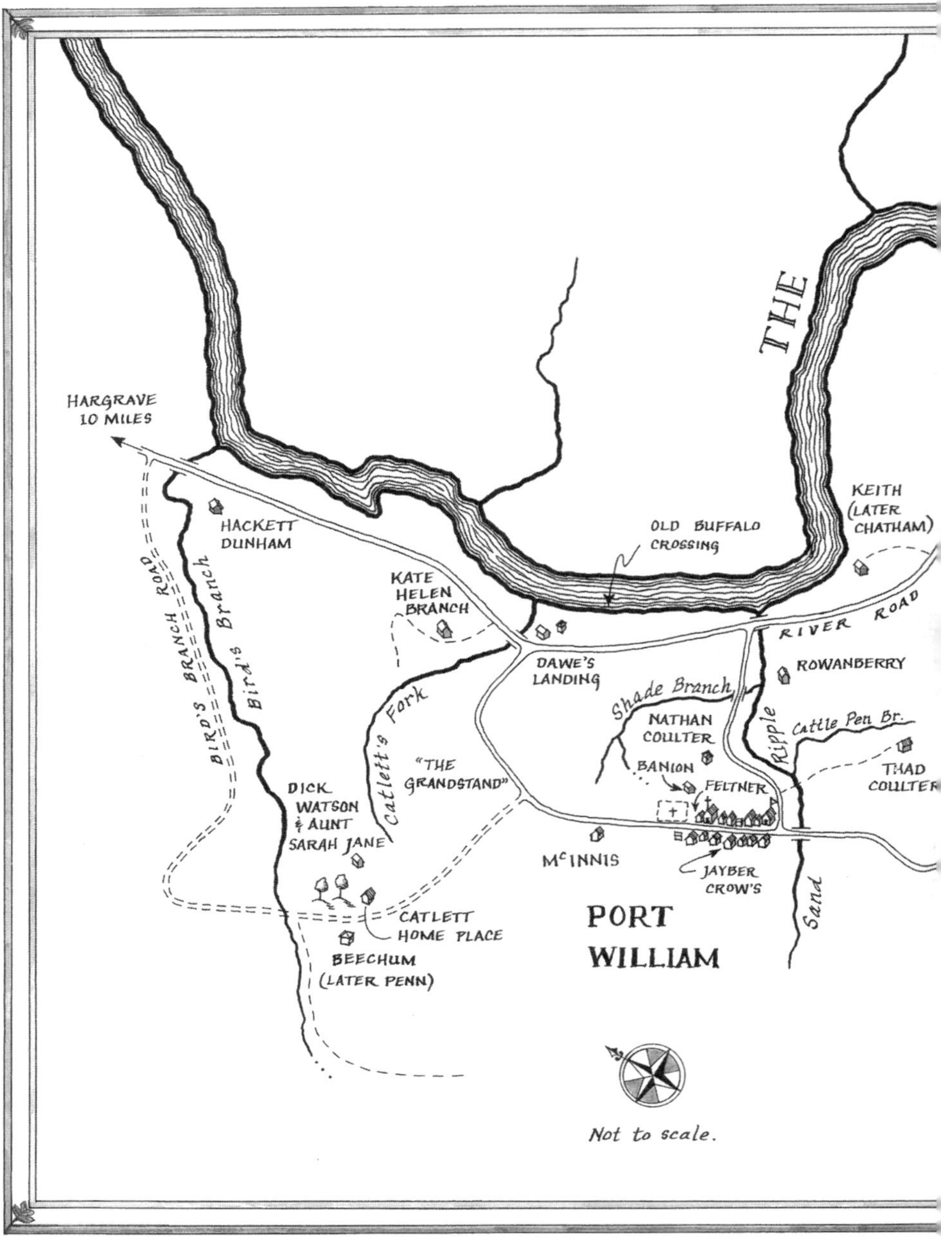
THE
HARGRAVE 10 MILES
HACKETT DUNHAM
OLD BUFFALO CROSSING
KEITH (LATER CHATHAM)
KATE HELEN BRANCH
RIVER ROAD
BIRD'S BRANCH ROAD
Bird's Branch
DAWE'S LANDING
ROWANBERRY
Shade Branch
Catlett's Fork
NATHAN COULTER
Cattle Pen Br.
Ripple
"THE GRANDSTAND"
BANION
FELTNER
THAD COULTER
DICK WATSON & AUNT SARAH JANE
McINNIS
JAYBER CROW'S
Sand
CATLETT HOME PLACE
PORT WILLIAM
BEECHUM (LATER PENN)
Not to scale.